W9-AGD-181

One glance told the Earl that the young woman was an aristocrat.

There was no mistaking the small, slight figure and the face that might have been a model for Boucher.

Her hair was dark, and her skin was very light.

Her eyes seemed to fill the whole of her fine-featured face.

She sank down in a very elegant and graceful curtsy.

"May I introduce, *Monsieur*," the old woman said, "*la Comtesse* Lynetta de Marigny."

The Earl bowed formally as the old woman continued:

"I beg of you, *Monsieur*, to save her life!"

The Earl looked surprised.

"Save her life?" he repeated. "But the Revolution is over."

"Not here, *Monsieur*!"

A Camfield Novel of Love
by Barbara Cartland

———

"*Barbara Cartland's novels are all distinguished by their intelligence, good sense, and good nature...*"

— ROMANTIC TIMES

"*Who could give better advice on how to keep your romance going strong than the world's most famous romance novelist, Barbara Cartland?*"

— THE STAR

Dearest Reader,

Camfield Novels of Love mark a very exciting era of my books with Jove. They have already published nearly two hundred of my titles since they became my first publisher in America, and now all my original paperback romances in the future will be published exclusively by them.

As you already know, Camfield Place in Hertfordshire is my home, which originally existed in 1275, but was rebuilt in 1867 by the grandfather of Beatrix Potter.

It was here in this lovely house, with the best view in the county, that she wrote *The Tale of Peter Rabbit*. Mr. McGregor's garden is exactly as she described it. The door in the wall that the fat little rabbit could not squeeze underneath and the goldfish pool where the white cat sat twitching its tail are still there.

I had Camfield Place blessed when I came here in 1950 and was so happy with my husband until he died, and now with my children and grandchildren, that I know the atmosphere is filled with love and we have all been very lucky.

It is easy here to write of love and I know you will enjoy the Camfield Novels of Love. Their plots are definitely exciting and the covers very romantic. They come to you, like all my books, with love.

Bless you,

CAMFIELD NOVELS OF LOVE

by Barbara Cartland

Other books by Barbara Cartland

A NEW CAMFIELD NOVEL OF LOVE BY

BARBARA CARTLAND

A Knight in Paris

JOVE BOOKS, NEW YORK

A KNIGHT IN PARIS

A Jove Book/published by arrangement with
the author

PRINTING HISTORY
Jove edition/April 1989

ISBN: 0-515-09881-7

Jove Books are published by The Berkley Publishing Group,
200 Madison Avenue, New York, New York 10016.
The name "JOVE" and "J" logo
are trademarks belonging to Jove Publications, Inc.

PRINTED IN THE UNITED STATES OF AMERICA

10 9 8 7 6 5 4 3 2 1

Author's Note

I FEEL sad when I see the great empty Châteaux in France whose furniture was all sold after the owners were guillotined or went into exile during the Revolution.

The English were by far the greatest benefactors of the Revolutionary sales. The Prince of Wales, later George IV, and his boon companion Lord Yarmouth, later the Third Marquis of Hertford, laid the foundations of the magnificent rich assemblies of French Eighteenth-Century decorative art in this Country. They can now be seen in the Wallace collection and at Windsor Castle and Buckingham Palace.

In March 1791, the Parisian Marchand-Mercier, Daguerre, held a large sale of French furniture at Christies.

After Waterloo, many of the newly impoverished Napoleonic aristocracy were forced in their turn to divest themselves of their possessions.

Soon after the declaration of Peace, Lord Yarmouth hurried to Paris. On his return journey he found it necessary to hire a yacht to cross the Channel. He divided his spoils on arrival back in London with the Prince Regent.

The latter acquired, among other things, the fine Boulle cabinets still to be seen at Buckingham Palace.

chapter one

1802

THE Earl of Charncliffe, driving through the crowded streets with his usual expertise, was aware that everyone was looking at him.

It was not surprising.

His four perfectly matched horses were jet black and his Phaeton, which had only recently been delivered from the coachbuilders, was yellow.

He prided himself on being different from his contemporaries.

But he knew that within a few months quite a number of the Bucks who modelled themselves on him would have Phaetons in the same colour.

They would copy it as they copied the way he tied his cravats.

They forced their tailors to emulate the cut of his coats, their valets the polish on his Hessian boots.

The Earl was extremely fastidious about his appearance which, added to his handsome looks, captured the heart of every woman he met.

He rather enjoyed being called a roué, although he often thought cynically that he was more often seduced than allowed to be the seducer.

Now for the first time he was courting instead of being courted.

He had inherited his title and vast possessions at what his relations called 'an unfortunately early age.'

Since then he had been begged, bullied, and pressured to be married.

Charn, the family seat, was the finest example of Italianate architecture of Elizabeth I's reign in the country.

The materials had come from many different places, and the Earl liked to recount them to his guests.

"Timber from the estate," he would say, "bricks from the local kiln, slate from Wales, glass from Spain, and stone from a quarry near Bath!"

He did not have to add that stonemasons and carvers were brought from Italy to ornament the rooms inside Charn.

The works of the greatest artists of every period comprised the collection of pictures that was one of the best in Britain.

It was a fitting background for the Earl himself, as he always looked as if he had stepped out of a picture book, and was one of the heroes of whom maidens dreamed.

He emerged through the traffic into the comparative emptiness of the roads leading towards the North. He thought it was a pity he had not further to go.

Elaine Dale, who had captured his elusive heart, was staying with her grandfather.

The house was not ten miles from the centre of London, which of course to the Earl and his friends was St. James's Street.

Elaine was the daughter of Lord William Dale.

Her father, being the youngest son of the Duke of Avondale, because of his subsidiary position in the family hierarchy, was invariably in debt.

His older brother, as the heir to the Dukedom, had everything that could be spared from the family coffers. The younger members had to survive on a pittance.

It was of course traditional among the aristocrats that this should happen and Lord William complained continually that his pockets were to let and that he was unfairly treated, but no one listened.

That was until he realised that he had a treasure of inexpressible value in his daughter Elaine.

To say that Elaine Dale was beautiful was to underestimate her attractions.

When, by pinching and saving, Lord and Lady William Dale brought her to London for the Season, she struck the Social World like a meteor.

Her mother was Irish, which accounted for her blue eyes. In the Dale family tree there was a Scandinavian who was responsible for the pale gold of her hair.

She was older than the usual débutantes.

She had been in mourning for a year, which had postponed her making her curtsy at Buckingham Palace, therefore she had poise and was also exceedingly graceful.

She had a musical voice and was, if not well-educated, intelligent enough to hold the attention of every man she met.

The Clubs of St. James's hummed with excitement the moment she appeared.

It was the fashion for the Bucks and Beaux to like sophisticated women and ignore débutantes not only because they bored them.

They were also afraid that by some mischance they would find themselves married to one.

Elaine was the exception to every rule and had been declared an Incomparable the first week of her arrival in London.

She had been pursued by quite a number of eligible Bucks who until now had preferred to preserve their bachelorhood.

The Earl had at first been indifferent to what he had heard about Elaine.

It was only by chance that he saw her when he attended a Ball with his current fancy, who was a very fascinating Ambassadress.

In contrast to the flashing eyes, provocative lips, and erotic suggestions of the Ambassadress, Elaine looked like a drop of cool water in the heat of the desert.

The Earl was introduced to her and succumbed as all his friends had done.

What surprised him was that Elaine treated him quite coolly. It might almost have been called with indifference.

The Earl was used to having any woman to whom he was introduced for the first time stare at him. It was as if he had stepped out of her dream.

Then she would make every effort to include him in her life.

Elaine greeted him. Then she continued her conversation with the gentleman who was standing beside her.

The Earl asked her to dance.

She did not seem to understand that this was a rare privilege accorded only occasionally to some very exceptional beauties.

She told him without any obvious signs of regret that her card was full.

The Earl was intrigued and, if he was honest with himself, piqued.

How was it possible that this girl, whom he knew came from the country and whose father had not a pennypiece with which to bless himself, could be so offhand?

He might have been even more perturbed had he but realised that she treated all the other men who were fawning on her in exactly the same way.

It seemed incredible in anyone so young yet she behaved like a star who had come down from the sky to bemuse mere mortals.

But not to become too intimate with them.

Because he was mystified by such behaviour, the Earl had gone in search of Lord William. He was a member of White's Club, although he could seldom afford to come to London.

The Earl found him drinking in the Card Room, but unable to sit down and play because he could not afford it.

"I have just had the pleasure of meeting your daughter," the Earl said.

"Pretty, is she not?" Lord William remarked.

"I think a more appropriate word would be 'beautiful'!" the Earl replied. "But I have never heard you speak of her."

"What was the point," Lord William asked, "when she was in the schoolroom?"

He drank half a glass of Champagne before he continued:

"All I can tell you, Charncliffe, is that daughters are damned expensive, and gowns do not last as long as a horse!"

"That is true," the Earl agreed.

He would have asked another question, but he realised that Lord William was somewhat foxed. He was

5

also obviously intent, because the Champagne was free, to get more so.

"What I have told the girl she has to do, Charncliffe," he said in a thick voice, "is to get married; the quicker the better, as far as I am concerned!"

"Are you below hatches?" the Earl enquired sympathetically, knowing the answer.

"The Duns are hammering at the gate!" Lord William said gloomily. "Blast their eyes! They always kick a man when he is down!"

As if in his bemused state he was suddenly becoming aware to whom he was talking, he said:

"If you want to marry Elaine, Charncliffe, I will give you my blessing!"

The Earl thought this was going too far and too fast, so he walked away.

He knew as he did so that Lord William was relying on finding a rich son-in-law, and, as he had said himself, 'the quicker the better.'

Because it amused him, the Earl watched Miss Dale.

He guessed she would play off her admirers, one against the other, until she eventually found one rich enough to suit herself and her father.

He knew if that was the case there would be no better candidate for being first past the winning post than himself.

The stories of his wealth were not exaggerated.

He owned Charn, with its five thousand acres of good Oxfordshire soil.

He also had the largest and most distinguished house in Berkeley Square.

He owned a house at Newmarket, where he trained his racehorses, and another at Epsom to which was attached a large estate with excellent farming land.

Because he did not dance with Elaine Dale that evening, and as the Ambassadress was very persistent, he did not think of her again until he heard her being discussed at his Club.

He thought the way she was being eulogised was rather ridiculous.

That evening he found himself sitting next to her at dinner at Devonshire House.

He was rather surprised that she should have been elevated to what was usually considered an exalted position. He remembered, however, that Lord William had always been a very special friend of the Duchess.

"Did you enjoy the Beauchamp's Ball the other night?" he asked. He was thinking as he spoke to Elaine that she really was lovely; it would be hard to express to anyone who had not seen her how she seemed to stand out amongst other women at the party.

They were nearly all acknowledged Beauties, and yet this young girl seemed to glow with a radiance that made every man in the room turn to look at her.

The Earl waited for an answer to his question, expecting her to say how much she regretted not being able to dance with him.

To his astonishment, however, she replied: "Were you there?"

For a moment he thought he could not have heard her aright.

It seemed impossible that he, the most sought-after bachelor in the whole of Society, should not be remembered by a mere chick who had just come up from the country.

"I was not only there," he said sternly, "but I asked you to dance!"

"Did you?" she asked lightly. "I am afraid I had to refuse so many invitations and it is difficult now to remember them."

Because it was a challenge he could not resist, the Earl proceeded to impress himself upon Miss Dale.

Incredibly he found that it was quite a difficult thing to do.

She listened to him and she laughed at his jokes. She made herself, he thought, very agreeable.

But at the end of dinner he was well aware that there was not the expression in her eyes he expected. She did not try to draw attention to herself.

Nor did she use any of the feminine wiles which he knew so well.

There was certainly no need for her to do so, yet it was what he expected and what he was receiving from the lady on his other side.

A week later the Earl walked into White's. When he appeared one of his friends asked:

"Have you seen the sweepstake, Darrill? You are lagging behind Hampton."

"What are you talking about?" the Earl enquired.

"I thought you must have known about it by this time, but they are betting on whether you or Hampton will win the 'Gold Cup,' which is of course the Incomparable Elaine!"

"I do not know what the devil you are talking about!" the Earl exclaimed.

"It is quite simple," his friend replied. "The Betting Book is out, and we are all taking our wagers as to whether you or Hampton will put a ring on Elaine Dale's finger before the end of June!"

The Earl turned and walked to where the famous Betting Book of White's was kept.

Turning over the pages he found the names of quite a number of his friends and the amounts they had bet on the contest.

At the moment the Earl was in second place and he

thought, as his lips tightened, that it was an insult.

He was by far the richer of the two and, for that reason, any woman should find him more attractive.

But he knew that it was important that the Marquess was the son of the Duke of Wheathampton.

He was however a rather ugly young man with a habit of drinking too much and being somewhat rowdy when he was in his cups.

At the same time, he had a certain success with the Fair Sex.

It was not only because of his title, but because he rushed his fences and laid siege to any Fair Charmer who took his fancy.

'If that is what she likes, she can have him!' the Earl thought.

However, when he realised that some of his closest friends who he had always believed admired him were betting on Hampton's success, he was annoyed.

He called on Elaine Dale that afternoon.

In the small and unpretentious house that Lord William had rented for the Season, she looked even more enchanting than he remembered.

She greeted him with surprise.

The Earl had the strange feeling that she had forgotten about him. It had obviously never crossed her mind that he might care to see her.

"Are you visiting Papa, or me?" she enquired.

She seemed so ingenuous that the Earl believed she was genuinely unaware which one of them it was. Nor did he consider her rude to put him into the same age bracket as her father.

He merely set out to make himself pleasant and she blushed a little at his compliments. When he rose to go she did not ask when she would see him again.

As he walked down the steps to where his Phaeton

was waiting, he had the strange feeling that she would not think about him once he had gone.

It was all so different from anything that had happened before that the Earl made up his mind that he would capture Elaine Dale's heart.

To be beaten at the post by Hampton was unthinkable.

He began to court her with flowers and an ardency which would have astonished the other ladies of his acquaintance.

His secretary in Berkeley Square could bear witness to the large amount of letters and notes the Earl received every day.

The majority of them were from married women who should have known better.

There always seemed to be a groom in different livery at the door, handing over to the footman billets-doux which smelt seductively of gardenia, heliotrope, or rosemary.

Now the Earl was writing his own and the grooms who carried them to the small house in Islington laughed amongst themselves.

"Real struck on 'er, 'is nibs' must be!" one of them said and the other stable lad replied:

"Oi don't blame 'im! 'Er makes all t'other women look like old 'ags!"

The two boys had laughed and the Earl would have been furious if he had overheard them.

Three weeks after their first meeting the Earl realised that the moment had come when he must express himself more forcefully.

It was rumoured in White's that Hampton had already proposed marriage on bended knee, and Elaine had replied that she must have time to think about it.

'Time,' the Earl thought, 'to see if I really come up to scratch!'

He had been very attentive, but he was aware that his reputation would warn her that he was unlikely to be serious.

When it came to a question of producing a ring, she would think he would be likely to run out at the last moment.

Because the members of White's all thought that was what he would do, the odds against him had lengthened considerably and Hampton was well ahead.

Tossing and turning for most of the night, the Earl made up his mind.

He really had no wish to marry, thinking his freedom was very precious.

He was, however, well aware that it was his duty to produce an heir, or two or three of them. It was unlikely he would find a woman more beautiful, or indeed more suitable, than Elaine.

Her blood was as good as his and there was nobody else in the whole of the Beau Monde who could grace the family jewels as well as she would.

He could imagine her wearing the huge family diamond tiara that made every other woman who saw it green with envy.

He had always liked the sapphire set in which the stones, of the deepest blue, were finer than those belonging to the Queen.

Because he was extremely experienced in women's dress, the Earl was aware that while Elaine looked exquisite, she did not possess many gowns.

The same ones reappeared, but with different decoration, which made them look different to anybody less observant than he was.

But, whatever she wore, it was impossible for anybody meeting her not to look at her face, her blue eyes, and the perfect curves of her Cupid's-bow lips.

The Earl decided that he wished to kiss her.

Although he had got as far as kissing her hand, he was too experienced to attempt anything more intimate. That would only be permitted after he had laid his heart at her feet and asked her to be his wife.

"Dammit, I will do it!" he said to himself. He would visit her the next day and would make her a proposal of marriage.

He learned, however, that Elaine had left London unexpectedly. He was told that her grandfather, the Duke of Avondale, had wished to see her.

For the moment the Earl felt annoyed.

Then he realised that if he made his proposal in the country it would be far more romantic. The Sitting Room in the house in Islington was rather squalid.

He therefore ordered the new team, which he had recently purchased, to carry him to Avondale House.

He thought, driving his yellow Phaeton, that any girl's heart would beat a little quicker at the sight of him.

His lady-loves had told him that he looked like Apollo driving across the sky. They added, like the God he swept away the darkness of the night.

It was a compliment he had heard so often that he had begun to believe it.

Although Elaine might not have heard of Apollo, it would, he thought, be impossible for her not to be swept off her feet at the sight of him.

The Earl was not actually a very conceited man, but he simply appreciated his own worth.

He would be very stupid, which he was not, if he had not realised there was no one in the whole of St. James's who could tool the reins better than he.

He knew too that he could outdrive every one of his contemporaries and also outride them.

It took him a little over an hour to turn in at the gates of Avondale House.

It was not a particularly attractive mansion; compared to Charn the architecture was inferior and the position badly chosen.

At the same time the Earl thought a little wryly, 'A Duke is always a Duke.'

There was the chance, although it seemed unlikely, that the more important title might tip the scales in Hampton's favour.

He remembered Hampton's ugly face and his rather stubby body. The comparison between them was ludicrous.

The Earl had taken the precaution of sending a groom early in the morning with a note to tell Elaine that he was calling on her.

As he drew up with a flourish outside the porticoed front door he felt sure she would be eagerly waiting for him.

Two footmen in rather badly fitting livery, which the Earl would not have allowed, ran a somewhat worn red carpet down the steps.

The Earl's groom had jumped down from his perch behind to go to the horses' heads.

The Earl, having put down the reins slowly and without haste, stepped down from the Phaeton.

An elderly Butler bowed as he reached the front door.

The Earl handed a footman his tall hat and driving gloves, and thought the large hall looked somewhat gloomy, which was because the pictures hanging on the walls needed cleaning.

He followed the Butler, who showed him into a large and overfurnished Drawing Room. To his surprise it was empty.

He had rather expected that Elaine would be waiting for him.

He recalled how many rooms of the same sort he had entered in the past. The lady upon whom he was calling had always been standing at the far end of it.

She was usually posed beside a vase of flowers and dressed in her most alluring gown.

When he was announced she would give a little cry, as if of surprise.

As the door closed her eyes would seem to fill her face. Then it was only a question of seconds before she ran towards him to fling herself into his arms.

She would say, and her words would seem to tumble over themselves:

"I hoped . . . you would . . . come . . . but . . . oh Darrill, I was . . . afraid you . . . might forget!"

"How could I do that?" he would reply.

"I love you, Darrill, I love you!"

The words would be spoken in a low, passionate whisper.

Her lips would be waiting for his and the warm and eager body, whose heart he knew would be beating frantically, was pressed against his.

It was all so familiar that it always made him feel as if he was on a stage and he was keeping to the script in which he had become word perfect.

To his surprise, however, Elaine was not waiting for him. He thought a little cynically that she was being cleverer than he expected.

Five minutes later she came into the room.

It was long enough, the Earl thought, for him to have to wait to see her, but not so long for him to be irritated by the delay.

She was looking lovely, no one could deny that, in a gown she had worn the previous week. It had then been decorated with blue ribbons which had now been changed to pink.

Her hair was arranged in the very latest fashion, but so cleverly that it appeared natural.

On her arm, as if she had been in the garden, was a long basket filled with roses.

She stood for a moment just inside the door looking at him before she said: "I am so sorry if I have kept you waiting, although you were kind enough to tell me you were calling. I did not expect you so early."

The Earl thought she spoke naturally; at the same time he was not such a greenhorn as to believe she had been in the garden picking the flowers.

She set the basket down on a chair, then walked towards the mantelpiece.

Because it was too hot for a fire, the Earl saw that the fireplace had been filled with plants and that the blossoms on them were a rosy pink, matching the ribbons on Elaine's gown.

"You are looking very lovely!" he said in a low voice.

She did not blush, but she looked down as if she was shy. It struck him that again it was exactly what she should do. Yet it was an act rather than a spontaneous reaction.

Then he told himself he was being quite unnecessarily critical and there was nothing he disliked more than a gauche girl who was unsure of herself.

"It was kind of you to come all this way to see me!" Elaine was saying softly.

"It was not so very far," the Earl replied, "and my new team made light work of it. I thought perhaps you would like to see them."

"Yes, of course."

He realised from the way she spoke that she was not really interested.

He wanted to tell her that Hampton was cow-fisted

when it came to driving and a second-rate rider who did not like a horse with any spirit in it.

He told himself this was not the moment to be thinking of Hampton, but of his own interests.

"I came, Elaine," he said in a deep voice, "because I have something to say to you."

She raised her blue eyes to his and asked ingenuously: "What is it? And could it not have waited until I returned to London?"

"No, it could not!" the Earl said firmly. "And actually, I thought the country, which I am sure you like as much as I do, was the right place."

It flashed through his mind as he spoke that he had no idea whether she liked the country or not.

He had only seen her in London and they had not talked about her home.

Then he forgot everything except that her eyes were searching his face and her lips, which were slightly parted, were very lovely.

He wanted to kiss her and felt sure he would be the first man to do so.

"What I came to ask you, Elaine," he said, "is if you would marry me."

The words came from his lips spontaneously and he thought, not as eloquently as they might have.

Elaine's eyes grew wide as she said in what was a sound of genuine surprise:

"I had no . . . idea that you . . . felt like that about . . . me."

"But I do."

He put his arm around her as he spoke. To his astonishment she put up her hands as if to ward him off.

"Please," she pleaded, "please . . . you must not kiss me!"

"Why not?"

16

"Because I have not . . . yet made up . . . my mind . . . and while you have asked me to marry you . . . I must . . . think about . . . it."

"Think about it?" the Earl asked in a stupefied voice.

He had never in his wildest imagination thought that any woman to whom he proposed marriage would not accept him with alacrity.

Now Elaine, who was fending him off with her hands, was saying:

"I . . . I did not think you were . . . serious."

"Of course I am serious!" the Earl replied firmly. "Very serious, and I think, Elaine, I can make you happy."

He thought as he spoke that it was unlikely she could be anything else when she saw how much he had to give her.

"You are very kind, and I know Papa . . . likes you," Elaine said, "at the same time . . . it would be a great . . . mistake for us to . . . rush into marriage . . . until we know . . . each other a little better."

The Earl was astonished.

"We have been seeing each other for the past weeks," he said.

"Yes, but not . . . alone," Elaine said. "There have always been a lot of people around us."

He did not reply and after a moment she said with her eyes cast down:

"I have heard of course what a success you are . . . and how many . . . women have been . . . in love with . . . you . . ."

"You should not listen to gossip!" the Earl interrupted. "And I can swear to you, Elaine, on the Bible if necessary, that I have never, and this is the truth, asked anyone to marry me until now."

"Then of course I am very honoured," Elaine said, "very . . . very honoured . . . but I must . . . think."

She walked away from him to the window and the

sunshine seemed to envelop her like a halo.

The Earl looked at her for a long moment, taking in the picture she made before he joined her.

Then he said:

"Be sensible, Elaine, I love you, and I know I can make you love me. Let us announce our engagement and be married before the end of the Season."

She put up her hands once again as if he was encroaching on her.

"I must think.... Please ... I must ... think!"

"What is there to think about?" the Earl enquired.

"You ... of course! You!"

"What about me?"

"I want to be ... quite certain," Elaine faltered, "quite ... quite certain that we ... love each other enough to ... be married."

"I would not ask you to be my wife if I was not sure you are exactly what I want," the Earl said, "and I think darling, you will enjoy being at Charn, and it will certainly make a perfect frame for your beauty."

He thought she was listening and he went on:

"Of all the beautiful women who have been the Chatelaines of Charn, you will be the most beautiful."

"Thank ... you," she whispered.

"We will get Romney to paint a portrait of you and I will hang it in my study."

"I would like ... that."

"Then the answer is 'yes'?"

Again the Earl would have put his arm around her, but she moved away.

"I ... I still want to think ... but I would like of course to see Charn ... if you will ... invite me there."

The Earl spread out his arms.

"Come tomorrow, and invite anybody else you like."

"You are so ... kind," Elaine said, "but tomorrow

18

there is a Ball in London which I cannot . . . refuse."

The Earl laughed.

"You will have to learn my darling, that, as your husband, I would be more important than any Ball."

"But this . . . one is rather . . . special."

"Why?" the Earl asked.

"Because it is being given . . . for me."

"By whom?"

"By the Marquess of Hampton."

"He is giving a Ball for you?" the Earl exclaimed incredulously.

"Only a small one, but as Papa could not afford to give one you can imagine it is very exciting for me."

"Of course," the Earl agreed, "and I presume I am invited?"

"I am sure James would ask you, if I beg him to do so."

"Do not trouble," the Earl replied.

Then, as he thought he sounded rather petty, he added:

"Of course, if you are engaged to me, Hampton must understand that you could not attend the Ball without me. Alternatively, you have every possible excuse for throwing him over."

"I . . . I could not do . . . that!" Elaine exclaimed. "It would be . . . rude!"

"Now listen, Elaine," the Earl said in a serious voice, "I love you, and I am determined you should be my wife. I will give a Ball for you in Berkeley Square, and another one at Charn."

Elaine made a little sound that he thought was one of joy and he went on:

"Forget Hampton and all those other men, and think about me, and how very happy I will make you as my wife."

19

"You are . . . so kind," Elaine repeated, "and I am longing to see . . . Charn."

"Then come home with me."

"When are you going?"

"As soon as possible."

Elaine looked away from him out into the garden.

"Papa has been telling me about Charn," she said, "and so has my grandfather who was a friend of your father's."

"I believe he was," the Earl agreed, feeling they were moving from the point.

"What Grandpapa said," Elaine went on, "was that Charn has everything that a great house should, except in one particular."

"What is that?" the Earl asked.

He could not help sounding a little sharp.

"Grandpapa was saying only this morning that, although your collection of pictures is unrivalled and your English furniture very fine, you have nothing French."

"French?" the Earl asked in surprise. "Why should I?"

"The Prince of Wales has a magnificent collection of French furniture at Carlton House."

"Yes, I know," the Earl agreed. "I believe His Royal Highness sent his Chef because he was French to buy what was being sold off at the Palace of Versailles."

"I saw it last week," Elaine remarked, "and I thought it very . . . very . . . pretty."

"If you want French furniture, you shall have it!" the Earl said.

He thought her eyes seemed to light up.

"Do you mean . . . that?"

"Of course I mean it! I am sure there still is a great deal of it for sale in London."

"It is obtainable in France now that the Peace has been signed."

The Earl stared at her.

20

"Are you saying that you want me to go to France to buy the furniture?"

"Would you do that?"

Elaine spoke eagerly and now she moved a little nearer to him.

"Would you do that for . . . me?"

"I will do anything you want me to," the Earl replied, "but it somehow seems unusual."

"I feel sure you would like Charn to be perfect, and if, as Grandpapa said, there is no French furniture, it would be very wonderful for me if I could be instrumental in introducing it to your house."

The Earl thought the whole thing very strange. Yet at least it was a new idea and he supposed he could understand why it concerned Elaine.

"I will go to France immediately," he said, "and bring you back a whole cartload of French furniture from Versailles, or anywhere else if it still exists."

He had the feeling that the sales at Versailles which he had heard talked about must be over by now.

He supposed, however, there would be a great deal of furniture from the great Châteaux still available.

Elaine was looking at him eagerly and he thought, with the sun behind her, she was exceedingly beautiful.

"If I am to go to France as you have asked me to do, then at least let us become engaged before I leave."

Again to his surprise Elaine shook her head and he thought her eyes were a little mischievous as she said:

"You are moving . . . too fast! Going to France will give me time to . . . think and when you come . . . back with some very . . . beautiful furniture for Charn, we can . . . talk about it . . . again."

"I find this very puzzling," the Earl complained.

"You are . . . trying to . . . rush me," Elaine answered, "and I am asking you to prove your . . . love."

She said the last words shyly. Once again her long eyelashes were dark against her skin.

"You are making it sound as if I have to slay the Dragon, or do one of the labours of Hercules to win you."

Elaine clapped her hands together.

"That is . . . exactly what it is, so please go to France and when you come back I will be . . . waiting."

"Are you quite sure of that?"

"Quite sure! I shall be here and I shall be hoping . . . that you are successful."

The Earl moved still nearer to her.

"If I do what you want," he suggested, "then I think the least you can do is to kiss me goodbye."

For a moment he thought she would acquiesce, then as his lips drew nearer to hers she put her fingers on his mouth. As she did so she bent forward quickly and kissed his cheek.

The Earl would have encircled her with his arms, but she slipped away. Before he could stop her she had moved across the room towards the door.

"Goodbye, and Godspeed," she said softly.

Before he could even think how strangely she was behaving, she had left the room and the door shut behind her.

He was alone with the uncomfortable feeling that he had made a mess of his first proposal.

What was more, he was more or less obliged to go to France, whether he wished to or not.

"Dammit!" he said aloud, "the whole thing is ridiculous!"

chapter two

DRIVING back to London, the Earl thought that everything was very different from what he had expected.

He could not believe that, having made his first proposal of marriage, he had been left in suspense with neither a 'yes' nor a 'no.'

He was not certain, however, what he could do about it.

Because he felt upset he went to White's Club to find his friends. As he went in he saw Lord William Dale sitting by himself in a corner at the far end of the Morning Room.

On an impulse he walked up to him and sat down.

"My Lord, I have just proposed to your daughter!" he said, somewhat aggressively.

The gloom on Lord William's face vanished and he sat upright.

"My dear boy," he exclaimed, "that is the best news I have had in years!"

He put out his hand.

"My warmest congratulations!"

The Earl did not take his hand; instead he said:

"Elaine has asked for time to think."

"To think?" Lord William exclaimed in astonishment. "What on earth has she to think about?"

"That is what I asked her," the Earl replied.

Lord William seemed about to say something pertinent, then changed his mind and said:

"I expect Elaine wants to talk to her mother."

The Earl vaguely wondered how Lady Dale was concerned.

Lord William slumped back in his chair and, after a moment, remarked:

"Well, I hope Elaine makes up her mind quickly, or you will be calling to see me in the Debtors' Prison!"

With a cynical twist to his lips, the Earl knew this was a hint he could not avoid.

"Let me make you a loan, My Lord, to tide you over."

Lord William was once again alert.

"Would you really do that? It is damned good of you, Charncliffe, as I have not the slightest idea where my next penny is coming from."

The Earl drew his chequebook out of his pocket and signalled to a club servant to bring him an inkpot and a quill pen.

"If I make it out for two thousand guineas," he said, "will that be sufficient?"

Lord William was almost incoherent.

"I always knew you were a sportsman, Charncliffe," he said. "I would rather have you as a son-in-law than any man I know."

The Earl thought cynically that that was not surprising.

He wrote a cheque for two thousand guineas, and signed it and passed it to Lord William, who hastily put it away in his waistcoat pocket.

"Now I think we should have a drink," the Earl said, "and in anticipation of our future cooperation, it should be Champagne."

Lord William was only too delighted to agree.

When the Champagne had been poured, he drank a glass quickly as if he was afraid it might be taken away from him.

After a short silence the Earl said: "I hear Hampton is giving a Ball for Elaine tomorrow night."

"Giving a Ball?" Lord William remarked.

"I have already told your daughter," the Earl continued, "that once we are engaged, I will give a Ball for her in London at Berkeley Square and another at Charn."

He knew as he spoke that he was bribing Lord William, as he had already bribed him with the two thousand guineas, but he told himself it was worth it.

Elaine was playing hard to get, and he had the unpleasant idea that the Marquess was still in the running.

He saw his friend Henry Lynham eyeing him across the room and as he took another sip of his Champagne, Henry came to his side.

"Celebrating anything?" he asked suspiciously. He was looking at the ice bucket containing the Champagne which the servant had put by the Earl's chair.

"Nothing in particular," the Earl replied. "Have a drink!"

"Thank you."

Henry sat down in an armchair next to the Earl. He was good-looking and well-provided with worldly goods, being the only son of a very rich man.

He and the Earl had been friends at Eton and their friendship had continued all through the years.

They had both sworn to each other that they preferred their unmarried status and the Earl was well aware that Henry's name had not been amongst those in the Betting Book.

He made a few desultory remarks about an invitation they had both received from Carlton House.

Lord William rose to his feet.

He finished off his third glass of Champagne before he did so, and put a heavy hand on the Earl's shoulder.

"Thank you, my boy," he said, "and good hunting!"

There was no mistaking the sincerity with which he spoke and, as he walked away, Henry asked:

"Is he saying that the Incomparable Elaine has accepted you?"

"She is thinking about it!" the Earl said briefly.

"Thinking about it?" Henry exclaimed.

The Earl thought the conversation was becoming monotonous and he said:

"I am leaving for France tomorrow or the next day."

"What on earth for?" Henry enquired.

"Elaine tells me that Charn lacks French furniture to which, again seeing it at Carlton House, she has taken a fancy."

"I do not believe it!" Henry exclaimed. "In my opinion Charn lacks nothing—not even a hostess!"

The Earl smiled wryly before he replied.

"That is what I intend it to have, but first, apparently, French furniture is required as a background for Elaine's beauty."

Henry was looking at him as if thinking he could not be serious. Then realising he was, he said:

"You never cease to surprise me, Darrill, and I have to

admit that the furniture at Carlton House is outstanding."

The Earl agreed, although he told himself he was quite content with the gilded furniture by the Adam's and Chippendale's exquisite carving which filled most of the rooms at Charn.

Yet, when he thought about it, he had to agree that the pictures, the girandoles, glass, bronzes, and Sévres china, besides the Gobelin tapestries that the Prince had brought from France, were certainly spectacular.

The Earl had a connoisseur's eye for pictures and furnishings.

He knew that the writing table by Charles André Boulle at which the Prince wrote his love-letters was magnificent.

He could say the same of the busts sculpted by Jacques Caffieri and the cabinets of Oeden with their ornate gold handles and marble tops.

He could understand why, because they were so ornate and so beautiful, they had taken Elaine's fancy.

That was what she should have and there was no one better than himself to choose them.

"Are you really going to France?" Henry asked.

"I certainly am," the Earl replied, "and the sooner I return, the sooner my engagement can be announced."

"Then she *has* accepted you!"

The Earl smiled.

"She will!" he answered confidently.

When he returned to his house in Berkeley Square he sat down and wrote Elaine a letter.

He wrote of her beauty and how much he loved her and he thought to himself that it was very eloquent. He also said:

I intend that we shall be married as soon as possible after my return, and this tiresome period of

27

*waiting will be over. I love you, and I know we
shall be very happy together.*

As he signed his name he could not help thinking
how many women would be thrilled to receive such a
declaration.

He sent it to the country by a groom so that Elaine
would receive it first thing in the morning.

Then he sent for Mr. Brownlow, his Secretary, to
plan for what he considered was a quite unnecessary
journey to France.

His yacht—the *Sea Lion*—was in harbour at Folk-
stone.

It was only when he was setting off the next morning
that he wondered what the situation in France would be
like.

The Peace Treaty had been signed at Amiens in
March. It contained a great number of commitments on
the part of England.

The Earl was aware that there was considerable op-
position in Parliament to the idea of peace.

George III's Government and the Prime Minister,
William Pitt, had wanted to continue the war. This had
already cost England £400 million, and had sent her off
the Gold Standard.

Their first reason was that they feared a greatly en-
larged France making peace with her enemies. Secondly, they were closely linked by a network of
friendship with French families in exile.

The war, however, which was previously popular
with the English people grew increasingly unpopular.
When the King and Pitt had a disagreement, over con-
cessions to Catholics, the Prime Minister made it a pre-
text for resigning.

He was succeeded by Addington—a doctor's son—

moderate and unambitious, who responded to the public demand for peace.

The Earl now remembered hearing that Napoleon was delighted. He had no wish to go on fighting.

Unfortunately, the War Party, having failed in Parliament, began a whispering campaign.

Greville described Napoleon, who was now the First Consul, as 'a tiger, let loose to devour mankind.'

He added that the French Government was a 'band of robbers and assailants.'

The Earl, who had always kept close to political affairs, remembered this. He decided, however, it would not in any way interfere with his desire to buy furniture.

He was aware that many of the items from the sale at the Palace of Versailles, which had lasted from August 1793 to the August of the following year, had found their way to England.

His Secretary had given him a list of the other big sales which had taken place at Fontainebleu, Marly, and St. Cloud.

"I understand, My Lord," he said, "that the flooding of such a large quantity of furniture onto the market so quickly was not conducive to producing high prices."

"Well, that certainly suits me!" the Earl said. "But why were the French anxious to sell so quickly?"

Delighted to be able to show his superior knowledge on this occasion, Mr. Brownlow replied:

"Your Lordship must have forgotten that in 1793 the Convention passed a Law to the effect that the furniture in the Garde-Meubles National in France was to be sold so that, and I quote:

'The sumptuous furniture of the last tyrants of France' might be 'put to the service of the defence of Liberty on the grounds of national prosperity.'"

"Of course," the Earl exclaimed, "I remember now!

And a damned silly thing I thought it was at the time!"

He had been much younger when this had occurred.

Now he wished his father had sent somebody to France to buy at ridiculously cheap prices the furniture Elaine admired.

Nevertheless, he was quite certain there was plenty left. All he had to do was to get in touch with the right people who would help him.

Fortunately, Mr. Brownlow was able to provide him with the name of a Monsieur Daguerre, the intermediary who had assisted the Prince of Wales.

Daguerre had for a short time thought it worthwhile to set up a branch of his French furnishing establishment in London. Later he had returned to Paris.

"Now I am all set!" the Earl told himself with satisfaction. "As soon as I have the furniture I can bring it back in my yacht. Elaine will realise how skilful I have been."

He was, however, in bad temper when he reached Dover.

It had been a long and tiring drive, spending two nights at a Posting Inn which he disliked.

He boarded his yacht to find that there, at least, all was satisfactory.

He had only owned the *Sea Lion* for the last two years.

He had made several successful voyages down the coast with Henry and some of his other men friends.

He thought that women were seldom at their best at sea.

If he wanted to entertain the famous Beauties who occupied a great deal of his time, there was nothing more comfortable than to take them to Charn.

In fact, the parties he gave in his ancestral home

were very exclusive, and an invitation was invariably prized.

The Prince of Wales had been the Earl's guest on several occasions.

He had been pettishly envious when he found that the food was better than at Carlton House, and the guests undoubtedly more amusing.

"The difference is," he had said bitterly, "that I have to scrimp and save and be continually in debt, while you, Darrill, can afford to live on a bed of roses!"

The Earl had laughed, but he had understood the Prince's resentment—even though it was his own fault.

His mistresses had spent so much on the furnishings and decorations of Carlton House that the public was objecting.

They thought such luxury was an unnecessary waste of money.

The Earl, however, had the idea that the magnificent collection which filled the great rooms would one day be appreciated.

He had been fortunate enough to inherit a house that was almost perfect.

He could therefore understand that the Prince enjoyed buying his own treasures whatever they cost him.

Now as the Earl set sail to cross the Channel, he wished he was at Charn.

'I will waste as little time as possible in finding what I require,' he thought, 'then return to London before Hampton—damn his impertinence—tempts Elaine any further. He is giving her a Ball—and Heaven knows what other sort of entertainment!'

He thought that whatever Hampton might plan it would be very inferior to any party he could give for her at Berkeley Square.

The much larger Ball at Charn would be unique in a dozen different ways.

When he reached Calais he was slightly apprehensive.

The hatred for the English which had been drummed up during the war might reverberate in some way on himself.

But the people in the port seemed only too willing to do anything that was required of them, as long as they were paid for it.

The women, with their red camlet jackets, high aprons with long flying lappets to their caps, and their wooden sabots, smiled at him.

The peasants working in the fields looked ruddy and well fed as he drove past them.

He had bought a reasonable conveyance drawn by four young horses.

The postillions and travellers on the road in the huge uncouth diligences were friendly.

Only in the towns were there signs of revolutionary destruction.

At Abbeville the larger houses were shut up and the streets full of beggars. The Castle at Chantilly was in ruins, it's beautiful gardens laid waste.

The Churches, now timidly reopening, were damaged, their windows smashed and the tombs desecrated.

However, when the Earl reached Paris it was difficult to realise that the country had been at war.

The Capital of the *grande nation* could be seen in its glory and triumph.

The Earl thought the new approach most imposing:

The Norman Barrier with massive Doric pillars, the long quadruple avenue of trees—the Place de la Concorde—and beyond the Consular Palace of the Tuileries.

He fortunately did not have to bother to call at the British Embassy.

It had been closed for the duration of the war.

Now it was too soon after hostilities had ceased for the two countries to have exchanged Ambassadors.

In his desire for haste he therefore immediately got in touch with *Monsieur* Daguerre at his Parisian establishment.

He was by now a comparatively old man, but only too delighted to advise the Earl.

He promised he would produce some excellent Boulle furniture for his inspection as quickly as he could get it together.

"I have of course heard of Charn, My Lord," he said, "and only the best would be right for such a magnificent setting."

The Earl agreed with him, and *Monsieur* Daguerre went on:

"There is in fact some furniture just outside Paris which I think would interest you."

"Where is that?" the Earl enquired.

"At the Château de Marigny, My Lord, which is only five miles to the South, and well worth a visit."

"I will go there to-morrow," the Earl said.

He had taken lodgings in a house which had once belonged to an aristocrat who had been guillotined, and had been acquired by an hôtelier who had welcomed him effusively.

The rooms were large and fairly comfortable, but not too clean. The service was appalling, and the Earl had to rely entirely on his valet for everything he wanted.

He therefore made up his mind within twenty-four hours of arriving in Paris that the sooner he could return to England the better.

He was thinking of the comfort of his house in

Berkeley Square, and it only came to his mind somewhat belatedly that the real reason for his wish to return was of course Elaine.

He found, however, that in Paris as in most other Cities, money spoke with a loud voice.

He obtained a carriage and some passable horses.

Although the coachman looked more like a pirate than a gentleman's servant, he could, the Earl found, drive fast but with some modicum of safety.

After an English breakfast, which Hunt had the greatest difficulty in procuring, he set off for the Château de Marigny.

The roads were bad and the Earl was only thankful there had not been any rain.

It took him, he reckoned, nearly double the time to reach the Château that it would have to travel the same distance in England on good roads and with his own superb horseflesh.

It was a very attractive Château, set in formal gardens which had been allowed to run riot.

The stone fountain, elaborately carved, was now broken, as were a great number of windows of the Château which had doubtless been shattered by stones.

Nevertheless, it was an impressive mansion built at the end of the Sixteenth Century.

The countryside around it was thick with trees which were covered with the green buds of Spring.

The coachman drove the carriage up to the front door, but there appeared to be nobody about.

The Earl walked up a long flight of stone steps to find that the door was open. He entered the hall.

It had an elegance which was very French, with its carved and gilt staircase and sculpted marble fireplace which was very beautiful.

Everything looked dirty.

There was dust on the few pieces of furniture that remained.

There was no carpet on the stairs.

The Earl was wondering what he should do when a man came from the door at the other end of the hall.

He looked coarse and unpleasant, and was dressed in what had been the uniform of the Revolution, but which was now, rather like the house, untidy and none too clean.

"Who are you, and what do you want?" he asked in an aggressive voice.

Speaking in his fluent and excellent Parisian French, the Earl replied:

"I have been sent by *Monsieur* Daguerre, and I am the Earl of Charncliffe."

"I am Jacques Ségar," the man replied, "and I am in charge of this Château."

"I congratulate you!" the Earl replied.

He was sure that the man was telling him that he had taken it over during the Revolution. But he was not prepared to involve himself in local politics, merely wishing to buy what he required.

He explained what he wanted.

Jacques Ségar, in what the Earl thought a rude manner, showed him two outstanding pieces of furniture which he was surprised had not been sold.

One of them, the Earl thought, was exactly what would please Elaine.

It was a corner cupboard made by Riesener. Exquisitely inlaid with a painted pattern in the centre, the feet and sides were gilded.

He was pleasantly surprised at the sum which Ségar quoted.

It was, the Earl knew, very cheap for so fine a piece

of furniture, but he was sure it was more than the Frenchman expected.

He bargained because he would have been foolish not to, and obtained the corner cupboard for what he knew was a quarter of its worth.

A large and impressive Reception Room with high windows overlooking the formal garden at the back of the Château was empty.

Except that against one wall there was a particularly fine clock/barometer.

Surmounted by a Cupid, the Earl thought it would be very appropriate for Elaine, and after some further haggling he bought it.

Two tables, four Louis XIV chairs, and a secretaire inset with Sèvres porcelain plaques were added to his purchases.

At midday Ségar said in an aggressive voice:

"Well, I'm off for my *déjeuner*. If you've brought yours, you can please yourself whether you eat it in the house or outside."

"Thank you for your permission!" the Earl said with a note of sarcasm in his voice.

Ségar, however, was quite unaware that his visitor despised him.

"I'll be back in about an hour-and-a-half," he said, "and you can tell me what else you want, or pay me for what you've already chosen."

He strode off down the steps and the Earl thought he was an extremely unpleasant man and was glad to be rid of him.

There were still a number of rooms he had not inspected.

But he thought he would do better on his own than with Ségar.

He smelt of garlic and was obviously hostile to any-one he knew was an aristocrat.

He left, riding a horse he had taken from the stables not far from the house.

The Earl's valet and the coachman then carried in the picnic basket he had brought with him from Paris.

Inside it was a pâté and several excellent cold dishes as well as a bottle of wine.

The Earl sat down at a table which had been made by a master craftsman, and Hunt waited on him.

When he had finished, eating quickly as he always did, he realised it would be some time before Ségar returned.

He left the room in which he had eaten and started to explore the bedrooms.

Most of them were empty, but in one there was an exquisite mirror hanging on the wall which was carved with Cupids and flowers, surmounted by a coat of arms.

The Earl knew it was the coat of arms of the *Comte* and *Comtesse* de Marigny, to whom the Château had belonged.

He supposed they had been guillotined.

Then as he stared at the mirror, he was aware that somebody was standing behind him.

He turned round to see an elderly woman with white hair who was clearly of a different class than Ségar.

She was tidily if poorly dressed and came towards him very quietly until she had reached his side.

"Please, *Monsieur*," she said, "may I speak to you?"

"Yes, of course," the Earl replied.

The old woman glanced over her shoulder as if she was afraid before she asked:

"You are English?"

"I am!"

"Then, would you come with me? I have something

37

to show you which is of great importance."

There was a pleading in her voice which the Earl thought rather moving.

He was aware that she was speaking perfect Parisian French, and was therefore well-educated.

He smiled at her reassuringly before he said:

"I am prepared to look at anything you have to show me."

He had the idea that she had spirited away from the Château something of value that had not fallen into the hands of the unpleasant Ségar.

Once again the old woman looked over her shoulder.

Then she went to the side of the mantelpiece and ran her hand along the white panelling which covered the whole room.

The Earl watched her in surprise until a piece of the panelling slid open and he saw there was an aperture.

The woman stepped into it, beckoning him to follow her, and just for a moment he hesitated, wondering if it was a trap of some sort.

Then he told himself he was quite certain that he would encounter no danger from the elderly French-woman.

He stepped through the panelling, which she instantly closed behind him.

It took a few seconds for him to adjust his eyes to the darkness.

Then, as the Frenchwoman went ahead he saw very faintly—and he was not certain where it came from—a light, showing him a long flight of stairs going downwards.

They were so narrow that he knew he must be between two walls of the Château.

He followed the Frenchwoman for a long way.

Then, when he was sure that they must be well beneath the ground floor, there was a passage.

Here the light came intermittently through small holes which made him suspect he was beneath the garden.

Perhaps near one of the stone balustrades that he had seen on either side of the formal flower beds with their box hedges.

The Frenchwoman walked on still without speaking.

They climbed up another flight of steps as narrow as the one by which they had descended.

At the top she paused, then feeling in front of her, opened what the Earl saw was a panelled opening into a room.

She stepped into it.

As the Earl joined her he saw that the room which they had now entered was small, with a low ceiling, and sparsely furnished.

He looked around and was aware there was nothing valuable in the room.

The Frenchwoman said in a low voice:

"Please, wait here."

She opened the door and he heard her whispering to somebody outside.

A moment later she came back into the room and brought with her a young woman.

One glance at the newcomer told the Earl without any need for words that she was an aristocrat.

There was no mistaking the small slight figure and the face that might have been a model for Boucher.

Her hair, arranged simply, was dark, and her skin was very light.

Her eyes, which the Earl realised had a frightened expression in them, were very large.

They seemed to fill the whole of her small fine-featured face.

She walked up to the Earl beside the elderly woman.

Then she sank down in what he knew was a very elegant and graceful curtsy.

"May I introduce, *Monsieur*," the old woman said, "*la Comtesse* Lynetta de Marigny."

The Earl bowed formally and the Frenchwoman said:

"You are English, because I heard you talking to your man-servant. As the *Comtesse* Lynetta is half-English, I beg of you, *Monsieur*, on my knees, to save her life!"

The Earl looked surprised.

"Save her life?" he repeated. "But the Revolution is over."

"Not here, *Monsieur*!"

"I do not understand."

The elderly woman would have spoken again, but the *Comtesse* made a little gesture and said in English:

"Forgive us, *Monsieur*, for bothering you, but my old Governess, *Mademoiselle* Bernier, speaks the truth when she says my life is in danger."

"I find that horrifying!" the Earl replied, also speaking in English. "Suppose we sit down and you tell me about it?"

He seated himself in an arm-chair as he spoke.

Almost as if he had given a command, the *Comtesse* sat near him on a high-backed chair, placing her hands in her lap.

Mademoiselle Bernier withdrew as if she was keeping to her proper place in the background.

"Perhaps I should introduce myself," the Earl said as the *Comtesse* did not speak. "I am the Earl of Charncliffe, and I have come to Paris to buy French furniture."

"I thought that was why you were here," Lynetta said

in a soft voice, "and I would like you to have all that is left of Papa's collection."

"Your father owned this Château?" the Earl asked.

"It is my home," Lynetta replied, "but it has been taken over by a cruel and wicked man."

"You mean Ségar?"

She nodded.

"I thought he was an unpleasant creature," the Earl remarked.

"He ... had ... Papa and Mama ... guillotined," Lynetta replied. "The people on our estate loved them and would never have ... hurt them ... but three years ago he ... took them away."

"But you were saved," the Earl remarked.

"It was *Mademoiselle*," Lynetta replied, glancing at her Governess from across the room. "She hid me in the secret passage by which you have just come here, and nobody else knows that it exists."

"You are lucky," the Earl said.

"Every day, unless I stay in that dark passage, I am in danger!"

"How?" he asked.

"Ségar knows I am alive somewhere and guesses that I am hiding in the Château or in the grounds."

She drew a deep breath and the Earl knew she was afraid as she went on:

"He is always searching ... watching ... bribing people to tell him if they have seen me."

"It sounds frightening!" the Earl remarked.

"It is, and I am afraid not only for myself, but also for *Mademoiselle*."

There was a note of terror in her voice as she said:

"If he finds me he will not only kill me, but also punish *Mademoiselle* in some horrifying manner!"

The Earl frowned.

If there was one thing he disliked it was cruelty, and he could understand what this young woman, hiding from a vengeful man, was suffering.

"*Mademoiselle* has been brave enough to ask your help," Lynetta went on. "I know it is a great deal to ask . . . but could you . . . please . . . take me . . . away? If I can reach England . . . I am sure some of Mama's . . . relations are still alive."

There was silence until the Earl said quietly:

"You leave me no alternative, so I must do as you ask."

"You mean . . . you will . . . really help me?"

There was a sudden radiance on her face that was very touching.

As she clasped her hands together, the Earl could see that the knuckles showed white.

"You will really do that?"

"I will do my best," he said. "But you are aware it is not going to be easy?"

"*Mademoiselle* has an idea."

"What is it?"

Mademoiselle Bernier came forward from the back of the room.

"I feel sure, *Monsieur*," she said in French, "that you will wish to buy the corner cabinet which is the best of anything left in the Château."

"I have already agreed to a price for it," the Earl confirmed.

"Then if you fetch it to-morrow, and the men are very careful how they handle it, the *Comtesse* could hide inside!"

The Earl looked at her in astonishment.

"There is room?" he asked.

"She will be more comfortable than she will be here if she is found." The Frenchwoman spoke very simply.

The sincerity in her tone told the Earl there was no doubt that she believed everything she was saying.

"Why is this man so determined to avenge himself on you?" he asked Lynetta.

"Papa dismissed him when he was young because he stole, drank, and was very offensive to the other servants. When the Revolution came, he saw a chance to get his revenge on all aristocrats."

"I understand," the Earl said. "And you really believe he intends to kill you?"

"He might . . . torture me first as we have heard he tortured some . . . of our friends . . . when he was . . . in Paris."

She spoke quietly and undramatically.

It was impossible for the Earl not to believe she was speaking the truth.

"I will help you," he said, "but it will not be easy."

"Please . . . please . . . take me back to England. I do not feel any longer that France is my country after what they have done to . . . Papa and Mama."

"We have to plan carefully," the Earl said. "If Ségar believes that you are trying to escape he will undoubtedly search any piece of furniture in which you might be concealed."

Mademoiselle gave a cry of horror, but Lynetta just looked at him.

Her large eyes told him more eloquently than words what she was feeling.

"I have a better idea," the Earl said, "but it might be more uncomfortable."

"Nothing could be more uncomfortable than dying at Ségar's hands," Lynetta said quietly.

"Are there any carpets in the Château?"

There was silence.

Then *Mademoiselle* Bernier replied:

"Yes, there are some. Quite a number that were not sold were put in a room at the end of the main passage. I saw them one evening when I was creeping around to find something we could sell for food."

"You mean—you have been hungry?" the Earl asked sharply.

"We have no money left, *Monsieur*," *Mademoiselle* Bernier replied, "and only by selling in the village the little things which I deliberately concealed before the sale, have the *Comtesse* and I been able to eat."

"If I take the *Comtesse* back to England with me," the Earl asked, "what will you do?"

Mademoiselle Bernier smiled.

"I have a sister in Lyons, *Monsieur*. We would have gone there, if it had been possible to leave the Château without Ségar being aware of it."

She gave a little sob and went on:

"He has spies everywhere, and *La Comtesse* can only creep out of the house at night, or sometimes, when we are sure it is safe, go up on the roof of the Château."

"I agree that this cannot continue," the Earl said sharply. "Now listen—I have a plan, and it would be disastrous to make any mistakes."

The two women looked at him, and he thought that the touch of hope in Lynetta's eyes was very moving.

Never for one moment had he expected to find this sort of situation when the Revolution was finished.

It seemed an extraordinary story.

Yet he remembered hearing that after the terror ceased there were still powerful factions in the Government and Army who violently resented any return to the old order.

The elections of 1797 had returned a Royalist majority.

It was, however, cancelled and once again there was a campaign against aristocrats and priests.

It was worse in the countryside.

No mercy could be expected from the Republican troops who, after a riot against them, shot seven hundred prisoners.

Over half were of noble birth.

He could in a way understand how the spite and hatred of a man like Ségar could remain with him for as long as he lived.

He was a killer, and, having tasted blood, he wanted to go on killing.

He would continue to murder even though many aristocrats had been eliminated and their possessions confiscated.

The Governess guided the Earl back along the dark passage.

He stepped out through the secret entrance into the room in which he had found the gold mirror.

He could hardly believe what was happening was real.

He looked at the panelled walls inset with brocade in what had once been the bedroom of the *Comtesse* de Marigny.

There was something horrifying in realising that a woman who must have been as beautiful as her daughter had been beheaded.

It had pleased the blood lust of the people who had been incited to hatred.

He could imagine the misery and terror in which Lynetta had lived for three years.

She had been afraid to go out into the sunshine.

Also she had been half-starved because there was no food to keep her and her faithful Governess alive.

"I must save her!" the Earl decided. "God knows it will be difficult. Just one false step and she will die!"

chapter three

WHEN Jacques Ségar returned to the Château after his déjeuner he found the Earl sitting in the *Comtesse*'s bedroom.

He was looking at the ornate gold mirror with its Cupids and garlands.

He had told Hunt to bring in one of the smaller carpets from the room at the end of the corridor.

He had seated himself on a chair in the centre of it so that he could admire the mirror in comfort.

Hunt was still with him, and, when Ségar came into the room, the Earl said:

"I like this mirror! But it will be difficult to convey it to England."

"It can be packed up," Ségar replied.

"Can you do that adequately?" the Earl asked.

He did not wait for the man to answer but added somewhat contemptuously:

"I suppose I shall have to pay more for the packing. It must be wrapped in linen, and placed in a wooden box, otherwise it will undoubtedly be smashed on the journey."

"It can be seen to if the price is right," Ségar answered insolently.

He then began to haggle.

But by the look in the Frenchman's eyes when they finally agreed on a figure, the Earl knew he had been over-charged.

He was aware that the mirror had not been sold because it was too large and unwieldy to convey from place to place.

"That, I think," he said, "completes what I wish to purchase."

He rose as he spoke.

Then Hunt came forward to stand beside him and murmured something in a respectful voice.

"Oh, yes! Yes, of course!" the Earl said, and went on in French: "My man has just reminded me that I have seen some carpets in another room, and of course the one on which I am standing."

"They're at your disposal, if you pay for them!"

Ségar spoke in a surly manner.

But the Earl knew he was determined to sell everything he could.

He was certain that the money would go into his own pocket rather than to the Convention.

Somewhat indifferently the Earl agreed on a price for the carpet on which he was standing.

As he left the room, Hunt said:

"'Scuse me, M'Lord, but I wants you to use this particular rug while you are in Paris."

He spoke in English, and the Earl said in an irritable voice to Ségar:

"My man says that the carpet I have to use in the place where we are staying is dirty, so we will take this one with us now."

He had reached the door and looked back to say sharply:

"All right, Hunt, pack it up and put it into the carriage!"

He walked on down the corridor, followed by Ségar.

He had expected that the carpets left in the Château were unsaleable.

However, there was one Aubusson which must have come from the main Reception Room, and had obviously been too large for the buyers.

He spent a considerable time haggling over its price.

He bought another which was very colourful, but was faded in one corner.

Finally they came to an agreement.

The Earl compared the notes he had made with those that Ségar had committed to memory.

It came to quite a considerable sum in French money.

The Earl, however, was sure that when he returned to England he would find that everything he had bought was a bargain.

He thought, too, it was furniture that would certainly make the Prince of Wales envious.

"I will arrange," he said to Ségar, "with Daguerre for a wagon to come here some time to-morrow to collect what I have purchased. He will bring with him a Note of Hand which will be honoured by any reputable Bank in Paris."

He thought Ségar might object to this and was therefore not surprised when he answered surlily:

"I want cash."

"Very well," the Earl said, "I will send the money and of course I shall require a receipt for it."

He then copied the notes he had made onto another piece of paper which he handed to Ségar so that there would be no mistakes when the wagon arrived.

He paid for the carpet he was taking with him in cash.

Then, without hurrying himself, he looked into one or two empty rooms before he reached the top of the stairs.

As he descended into the hall he could see his carriage waiting outside.

He stopped on the steps.

"Thank you, *Monsieur*," he said, "for your help. I should be grateful if you would oversee the loading of my purchases onto the wagon, especially the mirror."

"I should have charged you more for that!" Ségar said with the first flash of humour he had shown since the Earl arrived.

"You have driven a hard bargain as it is!" the Earl replied, knowing it would please him.

He walked down the steps and into the carriage.

As soon as he entered it, Hunt shut the door and climbed up onto the box beside the coachman.

They drove off and the Earl deliberately looked out of the window.

He appeared to be interested in the court-yard and the garden until they were some way down the drive.

Then he turned his attention to the piled-up rug which filled half the carriage.

"You are all right?" he asked.

As he spoke he started to open out one end of the rug which was lying on the seat beside him, and a second later he could see Lynetta's face.

"Is it safe for . . . me to . . . come out?" she asked.

"We have a long journey before us," the Earl replied, "and I think you will be more comfortable sitting beside me."

"I am sure . . . I shall."

He helped her up out of the rolled-up rug.

When she sat down on the seat at his side, she looked out of the window and gave a little cry.

"Is it true . . . really true that I have got . . . away?"

"Keep your fingers crossed," the Earl said, "but I think, under my protection, you will reach England in safety."

She gave an exclamation that was almost a sob.

Looking at her, he thought she was even more beautiful than he remembered.

Because he had arranged for her to be rolled up in the rug she was wearing only a thin muslin gown with a woolen shawl round her shoulders.

Over her hair instead of a bonnet she had a light chiffon scarf which was a soft pink.

It framed the darkness of her hair which had, however, silver lights in it.

The Earl saw that her eyes, which were the pale green of a mountain stream, were flecked with gold.

He could understand that it was a combination of her father's and mother's blood.

It made her look neither English nor French, but a mixture of both, which was very alluring.

In fact, he told himself, she had a loveliness that he had not seen before.

He was aware that the reason why Lynetta's eyes seemed so large and out of proportion to her face was that she was too thin for it to be natural.

He knew it was from lack of food.

"How can I thank you?" Lynetta asked in a low voice.

They had passed through the wrought-iron gates and were now on the highway.

"We will talk about that when I get you safely to England," the Earl said.

51

"*Mademoiselle* Bernier asked me to thank you with all her heart for the money you gave her so that she can travel to her sister in Lyons."

They had walked back down the secret passage and up the stairs to the *Comtesse*'s room.

There the Earl had said good-bye to *Mademoiselle* Bernier.

She had opened the panel a little way so that he could see them both in the light.

Although he was aware that Ségar had not yet returned, he said in a low voice:

"Remember everything I have told you."

"We will be waiting here until you leave the room," Lynetta said.

"Then open the panel and let my valet roll you up in the rug, which he will carry down to the carriage."

"You are so clever!" *Mademoiselle* exclaimed. "I would never have thought of anything like that!"

"I think, actually," the Earl said in a slightly amused voice, "that Cleopatra thought of it first, when she wished to visit Julius Caesar."

"I thought of that when you were first telling me what to do," Lynetta said before *Mademoiselle* could reply.

"History sometimes is useful!" the Earl remarked.

He smiled at her.

Then, taking his purse from his pocket, he drew out a considerable number of francs, which he handed to *Mademoiselle* Bernier.

"This should be enough to get you to Lyons," he said, "and if you will give the *Comtesse* your address, we will of course write to you when we reach England."

She gave an exclamation of gratitude and he went on:

"As soon as our Embassy reopens in Paris, I will

52

send you a pension every month, which will enable you to live in comfort."

He saw the tears come into the old woman's eyes and she murmured:

"God bless you, *Monsieur*!"

She curtsied and kissed his hand as she took the money from him.

Now, as they drove on, Lynetta said:

"I would have been very worried about *Mademoiselle*, if I had not known what she could do when I left."

"I do not want you to worry about anything, except yourself," the Earl said firmly, "and being a woman, that means clothes!"

Lynetta looked away from him and he was slightly amused to realise she was shy.

"I . . . I feel embarrassed," she said after a moment, "to come away with . . . nothing but the clothes I am wearing . . . but that was what . . . you told me to . . . do."

"You must admit it was sensible," the Earl said. "If you had taken anything else, such as clothes and cosmetics, Hunt might not have been able to carry you. If he had dropped something as he went down the stairs, even the mice might have been suspicious!"

Lynetta laughed, and it was a very pretty sound.

"I did not think of foolish things like that," she said, "but of being ashamed of my appearance when we travel to England."

"There will be plenty of clothes for us to purchase in Paris," the Earl replied, "unless of course the Revolution has made the French lose their habitual *chic*."

"Anything would seem *chic* to me after living in secret for so long. As I could only go out at night, I began to feel like a ghost."

"You will start a very different sort of life as soon as we are on our way home," the Earl promised.

It was only when they were nearing Paris that he began to think what excuse he could make to the servants in the place where he was staying.

They were inattentive and unused to looking after a Gentleman.

They had not therefore come to the door to see him leave in the hired carriage Hunt had obtained from what the English would have called a Livery Stable.

The Earl had not used the carriage he had bought in Boulogne because the horses had been tired after the journey.

Although he had been impatient to reach Paris, he had realised he would not be able to change them en route for anything so well bred or so fast.

So as not to exhaust them, he had therefore driven them the correct distance every day.

Nevertheless he considered it essential when he reached Paris for them to have at least two days' rest.

"I think the best thing," he said, after some deliberation, "is for me to say to the servants, if they are interested, which I think is unlikely, that you are a relative of mine."

Lynetta was listening and he went on:

"You have been visiting friends outside Paris, and have come back with me because you require a new wardrobe."

"That is definitely true!" Lynetta said, "but I feel embarrassed, My Lord, at . . . imposing on . . . you."

"You are doing nothing of the sort!" the Earl replied, "and as I came here to buy French furniture, no one can deny that you are a very beautiful piece of it!"

Lynetta laughed again.

"You flatter me, My Lord!" she said in French.

The Earl frowned.

"That is a mistake!" he exclaimed.

"What is?"

"For you to speak French. From now on, you must speak to me only in English, do you understand?"

"Yes . . . of course . . . I am . . . sorry."

"There is nothing to be sorry about," he said. "I am just thinking out our story and making sure we make no mistakes."

Lynetta shivered and he knew that once again she was afraid.

"You . . . you do not think that Jacques Ségar is . . . suspicious?" she asked.

"There is no point in taking risks," the Earl replied. "He is a very unpleasant man. It might strike him as rather strange that I should want to take one of the rugs away with me."

"Or perhaps"—he paused, to continue sharply—"when *Mademoiselle* Bernier leaves he will search her little house and find something that makes him suspicious."

Lynetta clasped her hands together.

"Now you are . . . frightening me . . . again," she said. "I have been so . . . terrified for so . . . long that I thought for one . . . amazing moment that I was . . . free."

"You are free!" the Earl said quietly. "But, until we have left France, we must both be on our guard."

He had not forgotten that old vendettas and feuds were still being acted out in parts of France other than Paris.

Emigrés in England had sad stories to tell of their relatives who had escaped death for years only to be betrayed later by some vengeful peasant.

He knew, if anyone identified Lynetta, that she might be taken by Fouchét's Police for questioning.

That in itself could be very unpleasant.

Having played the Knight Errant quite unexpectedly,

he had no wish to find himself defeated over getting Lynetta safely out of the country.

"You are English!" he said firmly so that she could make no mistake about it. "If I speak of you in France to anybody else I will refer to you as Lynne, which sounds English. Your other name is Charn, which is the name of my family."

"I shall be very . . . honoured to be one of your . . . relatives," Lynetta said in a soft voice, "but I would not . . . want to involve you in anything . . . unpleasant."

"I can look after myself," the Earl said, "and I understand that Bonaparte is anxious to be friendly to the English now that peace is declared."

"*Mademoiselle* would occasionally buy newspapers when we could afford them," Lynetta said, "and they said that the Peace Treaty was favourable to France, so that the First Consul had been congratulated on his cleverness."

"That is what I heard too," the Earl replied. "If the French follow their leader, they should welcome us as we are English, whatever they feel about their aristocrats."

"I still cannot . . . believe that Papa and Mama, who were loved by everybody, should . . . have been . . . killed," Lynetta said in a low voice.

"It is something you must try to forget," the Earl said gently. "What you have to do now, Lynne, is to start a new life and forget the horrors of the past."

"I understand what you mean," she replied, "and while it will be . . . impossible to . . . forget, I will try to . . . behave in a way that will make Papa proud of me."

There was something childlike in the way she spoke which the Earl thought was very moving.

Then she said in a different tone:

"I am afraid I shall . . . have to . . . ask you to help

me . . . find my mother's relatives when we . . . reach England."

"You have not yet told me their name," the Earl replied.

"Ford," Lynetta answered. "My grandfather was Lord Beckford, but I am sure he must by now be dead."

"If he had a son, he would therefore have inherited the title," the Earl replied. "But where was your mother's home?"

"In Leicestershire," Lynetta answered. "She met Papa when he was young and very keen on horses. He was invited by an Englishman to inspect his stable."

The Earl was listening. He knew a great many people who lived in Leicestershire.

He had often hunted there himself, and he was trying to recall if he had ever met anybody called Ford.

"Papa was a marvellous rider," Lynetta was saying, "and because everybody admired him, Mama was told a great deal about him before they met."

"And when they did?" the Earl asked.

"They fell in love at first sight and it was very romantic!"

"I am sure it was, but I am surprised your father was not already married."

"When he was nineteen it had been discussed by his parents, and there was an heiress from a family a little to the south of Marigny."

"What happened?" the Earl asked.

"Mama's family had no wish for her to marry a Frenchman. For a long time it looked as if her father would never give his consent for her to marry Papa."

"And what had his parents to say about it?"

"I believe they also disapproved, but Mama had a large dowry, and she also promised to become a Catholic."

"I can see that would have made everything easier," the Earl said.

"They had to wait for nearly two years while both families hoped they would change their minds, but it only made them more in love."

"You had no brothers or sisters?"

"No, and it was a very great sadness after I was born when the Doctor said Mama could have no more children. To Papa it was a tragedy!"

Lynetta was silent for a moment, then she said:

"Perhaps God knew best, because if they had had a son . . . he too would have been . . . guillotined."

"That is something you are not to think about," the Earl said severely.

"I am sorry," she said, "and I am trying to do what you tell me."

She lay back against the padded seat as if she was tired and the Earl gave an exclamation.

"I had forgotten," he said. "Hunt left me some pâté sandwiches for you because he was sure you would not have eaten much for your *déjeuner*."

He leaned across the carriage to find the luncheon box which Hunt had left ready.

When the Earl opened it he found the sandwiches, and there was also, he saw, a half bottle of Champagne.

Although Lynetta protested that she did not want any, he insisted on her having half a glass, and he drank some of the rest himself.

"I do not want you fainting on my hands before we reach Paris," he said.

"I am too excited to do that," she answered.

He noticed that she ate only two sandwiches and knew it was because, on the very sparse fare she and *Mademoiselle* had been able to afford to buy, she had grown used to having very little.

"If you wish to please me," the Earl said, "you must try to eat more."

"I think perhaps, My Lord, you are telling me that you do not like thin women."

"I have not said so," the Earl objected, "but you must be aware that you are too thin to be fashionable?"

"It did not matter when there was only *Mademoiselle* to see me in the daytime, and the bats at night!"

The Earl laughed.

"Now you will find there are a great number of gentlemen who will admire you, and a number of women who will say that your figure is what they want themselves."

"Do Englishwomen want to be thin?"

"It is something they find essential for the new gowns which, now that hostilities have ceased, are just appearing in London from France."

"You mean . . . Englishwomen like to buy the French gowns?"

"There may have been a Revolution and we may have been at war," the Earl remarked, "but all women have been concerned about is their clothes."

He laughed and continued:

"They could not acquire the French silk from Lyons or the ribbons of satin which they assure me are essential to their bonnets!"

He spoke in such an amusing way that Lynetta laughed.

Then looking up at him in what he thought was a very touching manner she said:

"It will be very . . . wonderful if I could have just . . . one new gown! *Mademoiselle* and I have . . . made what clothes I have, but I do not think anybody could have . . . described them as *chic*!"

"To-morrow," the Earl promised, "you shall have the smartest gowns obtainable."

Lynetta clasped her hands together and her eyes were shining.

The Earl told himself that one thing was quite certain when he took Lynetta back to England—she would be an instant success.

He suspected she would become an Incomparable, and he wondered if Elaine would be jealous.

Then he knew it would be best if he could possibly arrange it that no one should be aware that he had spirited Lynetta out of France.

'I will trace her family,' he thought. 'It should not be very difficult, and, if they are still rich and important, they will see that she is launched in Society, and will soon find herself a husband.'

As they drove on he was thinking that the fewer people they saw in Paris the better.

The furniture could be collected to-morrow morning. Daguerre could see to that, and have it conveyed immediately to Calais.

He was aware that that would take a certain amount of time.

He was therefore debating with himself whether it would be wise for him and Lynetta to leave Paris straight away.

The *Sea Lion* could take them across the Channel, then return for the furniture.

At the same time, he was sure it would be wise for him to see the furniture taken aboard the yacht.

He was well aware that neither the Captain nor his crew spoke French.

As the drivers of the wagons did not speak English, there might be some difficulty in communicating.

He was still considering what he should do when they reached Paris.

He noticed that Lynetta, who had been very quiet and almost asleep for the last few miles of the journey, had suddenly become alert.

She was looking out of the window with an irrepressible excitement.

"I had forgotten how big Paris was!" she said in an awe-struck voice.

"When you are growing up and you have been away from a place for a long time," the Earl explained, "it either seems much bigger or else very much smaller than you remembered."

"I am sure that is true," Lynetta answered, "but to me, Paris seems very big, and also rather frightening!"

"I want you to promise me not to feel too frightened," the Earl said quietly. "For one thing, it will show in your eyes."

Lynetta gave a little cry.

"You mean people might think it . . . strange and perhaps make . . . enquiries about me?"

"I think quite a number of people will make enquiries about you," the Earl replied, "because you are very attractive, but they will think it strange that you should be frightened."

"Perhaps I should wear spectacles?" Lynetta suggested.

The Earl laughed.

"That would be a mistake. What you have to do is to think happy thoughts, and your happiness will show in your eyes."

"I will . . . do as you . . . tell me," Lynetta said meekly.

The carriage drew up outside the house where the Earl was staying.

There were no attendants at the door as there should

have been and Hunt opened it so that Lynetta and the Earl could hurry up the stairs without anybody seeing them.

The Earl had rented the whole of the first floor, which consisted of a Reception Room, a Dining Room, and four bedrooms.

The Earl occupied one and Hunt another, which left a choice of two for Lynetta.

She chose the one nearest to his.

The Earl knew perceptively without her saying so that she was afraid of being alone.

If anything frightened her she would either be able to call him, or else run to him for protection.

He was rather amused to find himself in the position of being a tower of strength against unknown adversaries.

It was one he had not been in before.

Most women protested that they had to protect themselves against him, while they made every effort not to escape his arms or his kisses.

He realised that Lynetta did not think of him as a man.

To her he was a godlike creature who was saving her from destruction and the evil intentions of a killer.

She was looking round the Reception Room excitedly when Hunt joined them to ask:

"Anythin' you want, M'Lord? I 'spect you'd like an early dinner."

"What is more important," the Earl replied, "is that you should find *Mademoiselle* something to wear."

"I were thinkin' abaht that, M'Lord," Hunt replied, "and I finds out, tactful-like, the names o' the best shops an' they'll even stay open all night, if you pays 'em!"

The Earl smiled.

"Then what are you waiting for?"

"I tells the driver Your Lordship might still be wantin' 'im," Hunt said with a grin, "an' 'e, too, expects his *pourboire*, as Your Lordship's well aware!"

The Earl took his purse from his pocket and handed it to his valet.

"Help yourself," he said, "and bring a good dressmaker back with you."

"I'll fetch Your Lordship a bottle o' Champagne first," Hunt said, "and from all I 'ears o' the prices them Froggies be askin' for their fancy clothes, Your Lordship'll be needin' it!"

The Earl smiled.

Hunt's impertinence was something he would not have tolerated from any other servant, but the man had been with him for a number of years and he found him indispensable.

Nothing perturbed or upset Hunt.

He rose to any emergency with an enthusiasm which was infectious.

The Earl knew that he had enjoyed carrying Lynetta out of the Château rolled up in a carpet and if there were any more difficulties he would be only too delighted to help to surmount them.

He opened the bottle of Champagne and left it on a table, then disappeared.

Only after he had gone the Earl calculated that as there were at least three hours before dinner, Lynetta should have something to eat.

He rang the bell and, after a long wait, a slatternly servant who was employed by the hôtelier answered his summons.

"I would like some fresh croissants, butter, honey, and fruit," the Earl said.

"They're starting dinner downstairs," the girl replied in a surly voice.

"Fetch me what I have ordered," the Earl insisted, "and as quickly as possible!"

The girl flounced away.

The Earl thought the Revolution had certainly not improved the manners of French servants.

He wondered how long it would take before things got back to normal.

He had heard that the First Consul lived in considerable style.

Almost as if by thinking of Napoleon Bonaparte he conjured him up, for a few minutes later when the Earl was alone with a glass of Champagne in his hand, the door opened.

It was the hôtelier, who announced:

"Somebody to see you, *Monsieur*, from General Bonaparte!"

The Earl looked up in surprise and saw a man entering the Salon dressed in the uniform of a Colonel.

The newcomer saluted and said:

"Colonel Réal. I believe, *Monsieur*, that you are the Earl of Charncliffe."

"I am!"

"Then allow me to welcome you to Paris on behalf of General Bonaparte, who has just learned of your arrival."

"Will you sit down?" the Earl asked, indicating a chair. "Perhaps you would care for a glass of Champagne?"

The Colonel accepted it, then said:

"The General is most perturbed that you should have arrived in Paris without his being informed. He would of course have arranged for better accommodation than you have at the moment."

He looked round disdainfully as he spoke.

The Earl saw that he noticed the dust on the mantelpiece, that the fire irons wanted polishing and that the carpet had not been brushed.

"What the General suggests," the Colonel went on, "is that you should, *Monsieur*, be his guest at Tuileries Palace."

The Earl was so astonished that for the moment he could think of no reply. Then before he could do so, the door opened and Lynetta came in.

She had tidied herself after the journey, arranged her hair and draped over her shoulders the pink chiffon scarf that had covered her head.

This concealed the state of her gown, which had become creased from being rolled up in the carpet and was also, as the Earl was aware, of a cheap material and old-fashioned.

The Colonel rose to his feet.

Then, seeing that Lynetta hesitated as if wondering what she should do, he said:

"I had not realised, nor had the First Consul, *Monsieur*, that you had brought your wife with you, but I am sure *Madame* would be far more comfortable in the Palace than here."

The Earl drew in his breath.

Then with a quickness that his friends had always appreciated, he said in English to Lynetta:

"Let me introduce you, my dear, to Colonel Réal, who has just come from the First Consul, General Bonaparte, to suggest that we stay at Tuileries Palace with him, rather than these uncomfortable lodgings."

He spoke slowly to give Lynetta a chance to understand what he was saying.

He appreciated that she saw by his expression what he was thinking and, with hardly a pause, she replied:

"What a . . . delightful idea!"

"That is what I thought you would say!" the Earl exclaimed.

Turning to the Colonel, he said in French:

"My wife agrees with me that it is most kind and generous of the First Consul to offer us his hospitality, which we are very pleased to accept."

"I know the General will be very gratified," Colonel Réal replied.

"There is only one difficulty," the Earl went on.

"What is that?"

"We may be a little late in arriving. My wife has unfortunately lost her luggage on the journey here."

"That is indeed a tragedy!" the Colonel exclaimed.

"My servant is at the moment procuring some gowns," the Earl explained, "and when he has returned we will come to the Palace. But it will be after dinner."

"That will not matter," Colonel Réal replied. "The General and his wife, *Madame* Bonaparte are to-night having only a small party. I am sure he will be delighted if you and *Madame* can join us as soon as it is possible."

"Thank you," the Earl said. "Please convey my gratitude to the First Consul."

"I will do that," Colonel Réal replied. "And carriages will be sent for you at nine o'clock."

He finished his glass of Champagne, bowed respectfully to the Earl, and kissed Lynetta's hand before he left the room.

Only when they heard his footsteps going down the stairs did Lynetta ask in a frightened voice:

"What . . . do we do . . . now?"

"We stay at Tuileries Palace," the Earl replied.

"How can . . . we? And what will they . . . say about . . . me?"

"The First Consul will believe you to be my wife," the Earl replied. "Due to the war, the French have been out of touch with British Society for several years. It is not likely that anyone will know I am a bachelor."

He thought for a moment before he added:

"If pressed, we can always say that we were married just before we left England, and are here on our honeymoon."

There was a twist to his lips as he finished:

"We are of course buying French furniture for our home!"

"It is . . . dangerous . . . I know it is . . . dangerous!" Lynetta cried.

"There is nothing else we can do," the Earl replied. "It would be insulting to say we would prefer to stay in this badly run and dirty house rather than avail ourselves of the hospitality of the most important man in France!"

He refilled his glass with Champagne before he added:

"As it happens, I shall be interested to meet Bonaparte."

"Could you not . . . leave me . . . here?" Lynetta asked.

"That would certainly be an extremely stupid thing to do," the Earl said sharply.

"Why?"

"First because Napoleon would think you were not my wife, and staying with me in a rather different capacity."

He saw that Lynetta did not understand what he implied.

"Secondly," the Earl went on, "you would quickly find yourself under suspicion by the rag-tag and bob-tail in this place who are supposed to be servants!"

"And they . . . might . . . report me?"

"One never knows—if they become suspicious that you are not English, but French."

Lynetta gave a little cry of horror and, moving toward the Earl, said:

"I understand . . . but you will . . . help me? Promise me that . . . you will . . . help me and not let me do . . . anything wrong."

"I will look after you," the Earl said. "All you have to do is to look beautiful and appear to be a complacent, rather stupid Englishwoman who thinks her husband is wonderful!"

"That will be . . . easy!"

The Earl realised it was a compliment to him, and was what he expected.

At the same time, he did not intend Lynetta to know he was in fact rather worried.

He realised there was nothing he could do in the circumstances but accept Napoleon Bonaparte's invitation.

At the same time, it was always dangerous to pass off a woman as one's wife when she was something very different.

That of course did not apply so far as Lynetta was concerned, but he knew that he could not leave her alone.

If, when the Colonel had given him the invitation, he had said he preferred to be where he was, it might have caused a great deal of speculation.

There was always the chance that somebody, and that of course would be Ségar, would recognise Lynetta as the *Comte* de Marigny's daughter.

"Do you resemble your mother?" he asked abruptly.

"Mama was very beautiful," Lynetta replied, "but my hair is like hers, and so are my eyes."

'That answers the question,' the Earl thought.

He knew therefore that he had done the only thing possible in the circumstances.

It was a relief when, a long time later, Hunt returned in the carriage. With him was a very voluble and intelligent dressmaker.

While they were waiting the Earl had made Lynetta rest.

He was afraid that after the excitement of her escape and the journey, she might collapse.

He had advised her to go to bed and she had obeyed him.

After talking to the dressmaker he was not surprised when he went into the bedroom to find that Lynetta was fast asleep.

Before he went to waken her he asked the woman to unpack everything she had brought.

He had seen there were two or three very pretty evening gowns which would undoubtedly suit Lynetta, and two others which he could purchase for her to wear in the daytime.

Hunt had been sensible enough to remember that, having lost everything, Lynetta would require a nightgown and négligée.

These the Earl took with him when he went into Lynetta's bedroom.

He deliberately did not ask the dressmaker to accompany him.

He thought if Lynetta was asleep she might speak in French rather than English.

He guessed she would have closed the curtains to shut out the daylight.

He pulled them back but realised that Lynetta was still sound asleep, looking very young and childlike because she was completely relaxed.

Her head was turned a little sideways on the pillow.

Her hair, which was longer than the Earl had thought it would be, fell over her shoulders.

He was aware that, because she had no nightgown, she was naked beneath the sheets.

It struck him that her body would be very beautiful with small tip-tilted breasts.

Because she was so thin she would also have a very slim waist above her narrow hips.

Then he told himself severely that he must not think of her as a woman.

He had to concentrate on the task of turning her into

what would appear to be an acceptable English wife.

Because he did not want to raise his voice he bent near to her and called her name very quietly: "Lynetta!"

She started and opened her eyes to look up at him.

As he spoke he thought how easy it would be to bend just a little lower and kiss her.

He was sure her lips, which he knew no other man had touched, would be very soft and innocent.

Then he said almost sharply:

"The dressmaker is here!"

Lynetta began to sit up; then she remembered that she was naked.

Just in time she caught hold of the sheet and pulled it over her breasts.

The Earl straightened himself.

"I have brought you a négligée," he said, "and a nightgown to wear under it. I have already explained to *Madame* that everything you own has been lost."

Giving her a few minutes in which to cover herself, he ordered the dressmaker to go in to her.

* * *

In the Sitting Room the Earl said to Hunt:

"Pack my things. We are leaving here."

"Leavin', M'Lord?" Hunt enquired. "For England?"

"No, for Tuileries Palace. We will be staying with the First Consul, General Bonaparte, as his guests!"

"Cor blimey!" he exclaimed. "We does see life one way or anuvver!"

chapter four

THE dressmaker had brought with her an assistant and a large number of boxes.

The Earl had been sitting alone for only a few minutes reading the newspaper when the door opened.

Lynetta came into the room.

He saw at once that she looked very different in one of the new gowns.

The style had been introduced to France by *Madame* Bonaparte and had just reached England.

It was in the previous year, the Earl was to learn later, that Josephine Bonaparte had started wearing opaque materials.

They were cut in an original way which in a few months was to become the fashion.

Her gowns had high waists, short puffed sleeves, the

skirt falling straight and moulding the figure without stressing it.

It was certainly, the Earl thought as he looked at Lynetta, a fashion which became anyone so young and so lovely.

The dressmaker had robed her in a gown of soft green gauze. It was the colour of the buds of Spring, and the puffed sleeves were adorned with small blossoms and leaves.

She looked, he thought, like Persephone, coming back to the world after the darkness of Winter.

Then he told himself he was being poetical, which was out of character.

He realised she was looking at him, waiting for his verdict on her appearance.

"Charming," he said. "Keep it, and wear it this evening. Buy yourself some day gowns and at least three or four for the evening."

He thought she was about to argue; but she changed her mind and disappeared.

He smiled.

From what he knew of women, she would enjoy every moment of wearing clothes which his experience told him were of the very best quality.

He had thought Lynetta could manage for herself, but she came back a few minutes later in another gown which was as pretty as the one in green.

There was a third that was most silver and made her shimmer like a moonbeam.

Finally, because he had realised she was too frightened to choose without his approval, the Earl sent for the dressmaker.

"I think we have enough to last my wife until tomorrow," he said. "After that we may require some more, but bring any that must be altered to Tuileries Palace."

He saw the excitement in the woman's face.

He knew that to get into Tuileries Palace might mean an introduction to *Madame* Bonaparte.

"See to it that my wife has everything she requires," he went on, "for there is no knowing when her own luggage will be found."

Stammering with excitement, the dressmaker produced a bill.

It was, the Earl thought, not as expensive as he had expected, considering the trouble she had been put to.

He had already learnt that the Revolution had been a tragedy for the shops who had been patronised by the aristocracy.

It had in fact been a disaster for dressmakers, hairdressers, jewellers, coachbuilders, and goldsmiths.

There were tens of thousands of servants out of work, as only a minority of them had followed their masters and mistresses into exile.

Many of those who were left were often boycotted by popular Societies as carriers of the dreaded aristocratic plague.

The Earl remembered hearing that artists had lost their patrons, and theatre managers had been forced to change their repertoires.

Perhaps the only exceptions were the Gaming Houses that had closed their doors, but not for long, as the Revolutionaries liked to gamble.

Having paid the dressmaker, the Earl learned from her that Lynetta was having a bath.

He went to his own room to find, as he expected, that one had also been provided for him.

He washed away the dust of the journey.

Yet his mind was occupied with wondering how dangerous it was to stay in the Tuileries with his supposed wife.

He had been forced to act on the spur of the moment.

He knew on thinking it over that there was nothing else he could have done.

To refuse the invitation from the First Consul would have been an insult.

But he could hardly arrive with a beautiful young woman unless he was prepared to have her labelled as his mistress.

He could not go alone and leave Lynetta unprotected and terrified in the house in which they had been staying.

'I have done the only thing possible,' he told himself reassuringly.

He knew he must prepare Lynetta very carefully so that she did not make any mistakes.

Hunt helped him into his evening clothes, with silk stockings and satin knee-breeches.

Because he was dining with the First Consul, he wore just three of his more spectacular decorations.

He waited for Lynetta in the Sitting Room.

When she came in wearing the green gown he thought that any man would be proud to call her his wife.

She walked slowly towards him with a stole that matched her gown draped over her arms, which made her look more graceful than ever.

She looked at him anxiously.

On her head she had a wreath of small flowers which copied those on her sleeves.

It would prevent anybody from knowing her hair had not been arranged by a fashionable hairdresser.

"Do I look all right?" Lynetta asked, as the Earl did not speak.

"You look very lovely!" he answered, "as I am sure

any number of Frenchman will tell you most eloquently!"

He spoke teasingly, and he thought Lynetta would
laugh. Instead she said nervously:

"You realise, because during the Revolution Papa
and Mama gave no parties, that I have never been to
one?"

"Then it will be a new experience," the Earl said,
"and you must not be frightened."

Because he knew that was impossible, he said:

"Do not worry, the French think the English have no
polish and are by no means as elegant as they are."

His eyes were twinkling as he went on:

"They will expect you to be uncouth, gauche, and
not to appreciate the art of conversation, so anything
different will just surprise them."

Now Lynetta laughed.

"You are very scathing about the English!"

"I, of course, do not agree with any of that!" the Earl
said. "I am only telling you what your French ancestors
would think."

"My ancestors, if they were alive," Lynetta said with
unexpected dignity, "would not be concerned with the
opinion of a Corsican Corporal!"

The Earl laughed, and it was a spontaneous sound.

Then he said:

"For Heaven's sake, be careful! If you speak like that
we shall doubtless be carried off to the Bastille!"

He was teasing her, but Lynetta went pale.

"I am . . . sorry," she said, "it is just that . . ."

"I know," the Earl interrupted, "but remember that
you are English, and although slightly suspicious of the
French, who were so recently our enemies, you are glad
that the war is over."

"Yes, of course," Lynetta said meekly, "and I shall speak as little as possible."

"That is sensible," the Earl agreed.

Hunt brought in their dinner, having supervised it downstairs. It was better than the Earl had anticipated.

Knowing that Lynetta had almost starved, he realised that she had a lot of hungry days to make up.

Yet he knew it would be a mistake for her to eat too much too quickly.

As Hunt brought in one course, then disappeared downstairs to see to the next, the Earl said quietly:

"Before we go any further, I think you should tell me exactly what has happened in your life, so that I know your background. Then we can forget it."

Lynetta looked at him and after a moment she said:

"Papa had always been happy in the country with his horses, and after he married Mama, they seldom went to Paris."

She gave a little sigh as she continued:

"The Château always seemed to be filled with sunshine. There were children of my own age to play with, friends who lived nearby, and relations who came to stay."

Her eyes darkened as she said:

"When the Terror started we could hardly believe that the reports we heard from Paris were true. Although Papa was a little worried, he thought, because our village was so small and unimportant, that we would be forgotten."

"And so you were," the Earl said.

"Yes, but as a precaution, although Papa thought it unnecessary, he told me the secret of the hidden passage."

"Did no one else know of it?" the Earl enquired.

"No one!" Lynetta said. "And Papa said that if he

76

had had a son I should have been left in ignorance."

"Why was it made?" the Earl asked.

To his surprise, Lynetta did not answer for a moment.

Then her cheeks flushed and she looked away from him shyly before she said in a hesitating little voice:

"It . . . it may . . . shock you to . . . know that."

There was a twist to the Earl's lips as he thought it very unlikely that anything Lynetta could say would shock him, but he said quietly:

"It is something I would like to know."

"My great-grandfather who built the Château was very unhappily married," Lynetta said. "He therefore lived on one side of the house and his wife on the other."

She paused and the colour in her cheeks heightened as she said in a whisper:

"He . . . built the passage . . . for a lady whom he . . . loved."

"I understand," the Earl said.

He thought the *Comte* de Marigny had certainly found amusement without having to exert himself.

"When *Mademoiselle* Bernier came to teach me," Lynetta went on, "Papa gave her the cottage which had been built by my great-grandfather, but of course she did not know of the passage until I was obliged to use it."

"How did that happen?" the Earl asked.

"When the Terror seemed to be over, we thought we need no longer be afraid, and everything would return to normal."

The Earl saw the pain in her eyes as she went on:

"Then one day . . . one of our servants . . . who was devoted to Papa and Mama . . . burst into the Dining Room to say that . . . Jacques Ségar was marching

77

towards the house with a horde of rough men!"

"It must have been horrifying!" the Earl remarked.

"We were just finishing our evening meal," Lynetta went on. "Papa jumped up from the table and said to me: 'Go at once to the secret passage in Mama's bedroom! Go quickly!'

"I started to obey him and he said to Mama:

'You too, my darling!'

"She smiled at him and, putting her hand into his, said: 'Do you really think I would leave you? If you are to die, then I will . . . die with . . . you!'"

Lynetta's voice broke on the last words and the Earl waited for her to go on because he felt he had to know the rest.

"I was . . . waiting in the doorway," Lynetta said after a moment, "and Papa said:

'Go, Lynetta! Go, as I tell you to do!' and I had to obey him."

"So you hid in the passage," the Earl said. "What happened then?"

"I waited for a long time, listening to the shouts, coarse voices, and the sound of the windows being smashed as they threw stones. Afterwards . . ."

Her voice trembled, but she continued:

"Afterwards I learnt that . . . Papa had . . . faced them defiantly . . . and finally they . . . carried him and Mama . . . away. They were . . . guillotined a week later . . . not in Paris . . . but in a Market Town that is only a few miles from the Château."

"What did you do?" the Earl asked.

"A long time later . . . I let myself into *Mademoiselle* Bernier's cottage. She had been too frightened to come out when she heard the shouts of Ségar and his followers."

"She must have been very glad to see you!"

"She was wonderful!" Lynetta said. "Fortunately Papa had not moved the money he had put in the passage at the beginning of the Terror."

"So you had some money," the Earl remarked.

"It lasted until the end of last year," Lynetta said. "Then, when *Mademoiselle* found out that Jacques Ségar was intending to have a sale of the contents of the house, she took from the Château a number of *objets d'art*, pieces of china, and miniatures."

She gave a deep sigh as she continued: "The people in the village bought them from her when she went shopping. But because she had to do it in secret and at night, they paid very little. For some of the things we only received food."

"And you were hungry!"

"Now I no longer feel I have a hole in the middle of my body!" Lynetta replied.

He smiled. "It is something you shall never feel again," he said, "that I promise you!"

He looked at her for a long moment, and added:

"I also hope never to see fear in your eyes, as I saw it when I first met you."

"I was frightened," Lynetta admitted, "in case *Mademoiselle* had made a mistake and you would betray me to Ségar."

"I hope you soon realised that was something I would never do!"

"You have been so kind . . . so wonderful!" Lynetta said, "but now I am . . . afraid to go to the . . . Tuileries."

"I can understand that," the Earl said. "At the same time, you realise you will be safer there than anywhere else. Ségar can hardly threaten you when you are a guest of the First Consul!"

"Supposing they . . . realise I am . . . not your . . . wife?" Lynetta asked in a small voice.

"I have thought out a story, and you can tell me if you can find any flaws in it," the Earl replied.

Lynetta clasped her hands together and her eyes were on his face as he started.

"We were married just before we left England. Because you had been ill, which accounts for you being so thin, we had a very quiet wedding, then set off on our honeymoon."

He thought Lynetta looked a little shy, and he went on:

"Unfortunately, when your luggage was being brought from my yacht, your trunk was dropped in the water, and, in the commotion which ensued, your other trunks that should have been carried from our cabin were forgotten. You therefore had only a few necessities until we reached Paris."

"A very few," Lynetta smiled.

"That is our excuse for arriving late at the Palace," the Earl said, "which I am sure *Madame* Bonaparte will appreciate."

He paused and added:

"We are buying French furniture on our honeymoon because one of our relatives gave us a considerable sum of money as a wedding present with which to purchase it."

"That is clever!" Lynetta exclaimed. "You have thought of everything!"

"I hope so," the Earl replied, "But you must be prepared to improvise if you are asked any awkward questions."

"You will have to answer . . . for me," Lynetta said, "otherwise I may . . . make a . . . mistake."

"You know I will look after you and protect you," the Earl replied. "They will expect you to be quiet and shy because you are so young."

He smiled before he added:

"Perhaps it would have been more sensible to pretend you were my daughter!"

"But that is ridiculous . . ." Lynetta objected, then realised he was teasing her. "I . . . I could have been . . . your sister."

"That would be dangerous!" the Earl said. "I do not have a sister, and if there are any English people there, they might accuse me of lying."

He knew that they would accuse me of foisting his mistress off on the First Consul! That would certainly cause a scandal.

Lynetta, however, just said vaguely:

"Of course I understand, and I am very proud to pretend to be . . . your wife when you are so . . . important."

"What we have to do," the Earl said, "is to make sure that everybody believes us, and we will leave as soon as we possibly can."

"Yes . . . please let us . . . do that!" Lynetta agreed.

Hunt brought in the coffee, and the Earl said:

"I think the carriages should be here soon, and as I already told you, Hunt, that *Mademoiselle la Comtesse* is to be my wife for as long as we are at the Palace, the fewer questions you answer about her the better!"

"Leave it ter me, M'Lord," Hunt said. "I'm a clam when I don't 'ave to say nothin', an', as Your Lordship well knows, I talks no French unless it suits me!"

The Earl knew this was true.

Hunt knew enough French to get by, but he could be stubbornly English when confronted with a situation he did not choose to understand.

By some magic of his own, Hunt produced a trunk for Lynetta's clothes and when the meal was over he packed everything that had come from the dressmaker's.

The Earl was aware that Bonaparte did not speak English.

He was just telling Lynetta to pronounce some French words in an English manner and try not to sound too Parisian when Hunt opened the door.

"I've jus' thought o' somethin', M'Lord," he said, "an' I bet you've forgotten it!"

"What is that, Hunt?"

"A weddin' ring!" Hunt replied.

"You are quite right!" the Earl agreed. "I had forgotten it!"

"I thinks I can buy one from a maid downstairs," Hunt suggested.

"As it is very important, I hope you can!" the Earl answered.

He was frowning.

Lynetta knew as well as Hunt that he was annoyed at having forgotten anything so important as a wedding ring.

As his valet knew, he prided himself on being very efficient and attending to detail.

Hunt disappeared and Lynetta said nervously:

"I am sorry to be . . . such a nuisance. Perhaps it would have been . . . better if we had not . . . bothered you!"

"Nonsense! How can you say anything so ridiculous?" the Earl asked. "You could not have gone on forever hiding in that dark, eerie passage!"

"*Mademoiselle* prayed fervently every day that an Englishman would come to the Château. There were none at the sale."

"So I was the answer to her prayers!" the Earl exclaimed. "And it would be ungrateful not to accept the situation exactly as it is and make the best of it."

"That is what I have . . . tried to do," Lynetta said,

"and I shall pray very . . . very hard that I will not . . . fail you."

The Earl thought it was touching that she was thinking of him rather than herself.

Hunt came back triumphantly with quite a passable gold ring which he had bought for two *louis* from one of the maids.

The Earl made a mental note that while it might pass this evening, he would buy Lynetta a much better one to-morrow.

It struck him too that, as a married woman, she would have jewellery and after a little thought he said:

"I think we must explain that as we had no outriders with us, and as we did not expect to be entertained when we reached Paris, we left your jewellery in the yacht."

"That sounds feasible," Lynetta agreed.

"Tomorrow, I will buy you a necklace," the Earl promised, "and of course a decent ring."

"This one is quite all right," Lynetta said, looking at it on the third finger of her left hand, "but it is a little loose."

"Give it to me, M'Lady," Hunt said. "I'll make it smaller with a bit o' cotton, but you'd best keep your fingers closed, or they might think yer bridegroom's bin very remiss in not givin' you a ring what fits!"

The Earl thought Hunt was being somewhat impertinent but there was no point in reprimanding him.

Lynetta was smiling because she thought everything he said was amusing.

The Earl hoped that if he could not sweep away her fears, perhaps Hunt would be able to do so.

The carriages from the Palace arrived within half an hour and the Earl and Lynetta set off in style, leaving Hunt to see to the luggage and pay the bill.

The Earl had been quite prepared to find that Bonaparte had made himself comfortable.

Yet he never imagined that he would live in the magnificence he found in his apartments in the Tuileries.

There appeared to be hundreds of footmen in green and gold livery as well as officials in gloriously gilded uniforms.

There were pages wearing gold chains and medallions, aides-de-camp whose sole duty appeared to be to look splendid.

They walked along high corridors brilliantly lit and heavily carpeted.

The Earl thought with amusement that it was only a few months since the English had seen Bonaparte as drawn by their caricaturists.

He was depicted as an unshaven scaramouch from a Corsican hovel, burning, looting, and murdering.

Now they saw him as the greatest man in Europe, surrounded by all the pomp and splendour of Royalty, with half the nations of the world paying him homage.

The aide-de-camp who was in charge of them led them through double doors into what the Earl knew would be the Grand Reception Room.

He was aware that Lynetta, because she was frightened, moved a little closer to him, and he had the feeling she wished to hold onto his hand.

In a whisper which only she could hear he said:

"Chin up! Remember, you look lovely!"

She flashed him a little smile.

Then there was a buzz of voices and a glittering throng under the dazzling chandeliers, each of which held at least a hundred lighted candles.

"The Right Honourable the Earl of Charncliffe and the Countess!" the aide-de-camp announced.

It was then the Earl caught his first glimpse of Napoleon Bonaparte.

Although only five feet, six and a half inches tall in his stocking feet, he was broad-shouldered, and his limbs were well made.

He was certainly more handsome than the Earl had expected. His complexion was fair, its colour very pale yellow, and his brow was wide and high.

What were arresting were his eyes of bluish-grey, penetrating and unflinching.

When he smiled, his expression was unexpectedly charming.

"I am delighted to see you, *Monsieur!*" Bonaparte said. "I only regret that I was not previously told you were arriving in Paris. Or you, *Madame.*"

The Earl bowed, and Lynetta curtsied as he bent perfunctorily over her hand.

"Now you are very welcome," he went on. "I hope you will find that Paris has much for your entertainment."

"We are delighted to be here," the Earl replied, "although, as it happens, my wife and I came to Paris very quietly because we are on our honeymoon."

"On your honeymoon!" Bonaparte exclaimed. "That is indeed something I was not told, and of course we must celebrate by making certain that your visit is a memorable one."

He looked towards Josephine who was at that moment approaching them, and added:

"I shall never forget the ecstasies I experienced on my own honeymoon!"

The Earl realised he was speaking sincerely, although, he thought, rather overemotionally.

Then *Madame* Bonaparte was greeting them effusively and the Earl noticed she took in at a glance Lynetta's beauty and the elegance with which she was gowned.

There were a great number of people in the room.

The Earl enjoyed meeting men who had been only names for the last five years, the majority of them intelligent and witty.

He realised, as he had expected, that Lynetta was receiving many compliments. He noted she replied with a quiet simplicity of which he approved.

He thought perhaps because she was so young that it was her French blood that gave her a poise which no young Englishwoman would have had.

Considering she had spent the last three years in hiding, speaking to nobody except her old Governess, she managed to appear quite composed.

She seemed able to answer all the questions she was being asked without stammering, or seeming embarrassed.

At nearly eleven o'clock the guests who had been at dinner began to leave.

It was well known that Bonaparte wished to go to bed early, and disliked late nights.

At eleven o'clock precisely he began breaking up the party by saying:

"Let us go to bed."

There were few brave enough to ignore the command.

As they moved towards the door the Earl could hear them debating amongst themselves where they would go next.

From the few conversations he had had, he had learnt that Paris had quickly returned to normal.

As one man had said to him:

"The Palais Royal is back in business, the gaming rooms inviting customers, and so are the prostitutes!"

The Earl laughed, being aware that the English would find it hard to believe that so much had happened with such speed.

When the last dinner guests had left, the Earl found that besides themselves, only a few distinguished personages from other countries in Europe were staying at the Tuileries.

"I hope you find everything you require," Bonaparte said, "and tomorrow, My Lord, I would like you to attend a parade of my soldiers which will take place at eleven o'clock."

"I shall indeed be honoured!" the Earl replied.

An aide-de-camp was deputed by *Madame* Bonaparte to take them to their rooms.

To the Earl's surprise, they went down to the Ground Floor where *Madame* Josephine's bedroom was situated.

They were shown into a magnificent bedchamber which had obviously been furnished in the reign of Louis XIV.

There was a huge bed draped with curtains falling from a heavily carved and gilt corona suspended from the ceiling.

The pictures by Fragonard were exquisite, and the furniture, mostly Boulle, was outstanding.

"*Dormez-bien, Madame et Monsieur,*" the aide-de-camp said, and bowing with an exaggerated courtesy, he left the room.

As soon as they were alone Lynetta gave a little murmur of relief and asked in a whisper:

"Was . . . everything all . . . right? I did not . . . do anything wrong?"

"You were marvellous!" the Earl replied. "And actually I found it quite interesting."

He looked round the room and said with a smile:

"We certainly cannot quarrel with our accommodation. I expect Hunt is waiting for me next door."

He walked across the room to where there was a communicating door and Lynetta followed him.

As the Earl had expected, Hunt was already in the room.

He had unpacked his clothes into a huge wardrobe which was inlaid with mother-of-pearl.

There were two outstanding French commodes which the Earl thought he would have liked to own.

On one wall there was a mirror which was even more finely carved than the one he had bought from the Château de Marigny.

A number of gilded chairs were upholstered in the finest tapestry.

"Is everything all right, Hunt?" he asked.

"We certainly goes from rags to riches!" Hunt replied. "There's only one snag, M'Lord!"

"What is that?" the Earl asked.

Hunt gave a quick glance at Lynetta before he replied:

"There be only one bed."

The Earl stared at him. Then he asked:

"Did you suggest we might need another?"

Hunt glanced over his shoulder at the door.

"I would 'ave, M'Lord, but I thinks it'd be a mistake."

"Why?" the Earl asked.

"Because, M'Lord, there be a valet 'ere as was recently workin' in London!"

The Earl looked at him in surprise, and he said:

"He were with th' Frenchies who was sent to th' Prime Minister to report th' progress on all that talk over th' Treaty."

The Earl frowned, but he knew what Hunt was talking about.

"He were engaged, M'Lord, because 'e be English, an' 'is Master thinks 'e might be useful."

He paused so that the Earl could appreciate what he was saying before he continued:

"'E sez t'me, 'e sez: 'They talks about your Master when I were in London. I makes money too, on the horses 'e were running at Epsom.'"

The Earl did not interrupt, but he thought that this was something that need not have happened, and was in fact bad luck.

"'I didn't know 'e were married,' th' fellow goes on," Hunt related. "'They talks about 'im as if he's a real Casanova!'"

The Earl's lips tightened and there was an expression on his face which made Hunt say quickly:

"I was only tellin' Your Lordship wot this man sez!"

"Go on," the Earl ordered.

"I explains that you've just got married," Hunt continued, "an' after that 'twere difficult to suggest you should 'ave two beds on yer honeymoon!"

The Earl thought this was at least logical.

Then he realised that while Hunt had been talking Lynetta had gone back through the communicating door into the bedroom.

Without saying any more, he followed her.

She was standing looking at the bed, and he realised she was frightened.

"It is all right," he said soothingly. "I will sleep on the floor in the next room, and I am sure Hunt can find me some extra blankets and a pillow."

"The servants . . . might find . . . out . . . and think it . . . very strange," Lynetta faltered.

"We are clever enough to keep up appearances for

the short time we will be here," the Earl said gently.

"At the same time . . . it is dangerous," Lynetta whispered, "and I knew to-night that several of the people to whom I was talking were . . . surprised that . . . you were . . . married."

The Earl thought a little wryly that was what happened when a man had a reputation for being a *roué*.

And after all, who would appreciate that more than the French?

"I have an idea," Lynetta said in a very low voice, "but it may . . . shock you."

"I think that unlikely," the Earl remarked, "so let me hear what it is."

Lynetta's eyes flickered so that he knew she was shy and also blushing.

"I . . . I thought . . ." she said in a voice he could hardly hear, "that if I . . . slept on one side of the . . . bed . . . inside the sheet, and you . . . slept on the outside . . . with the eiderdown to keep you warm . . . the housemaids, when they saw the room in the morning . . . would be quite certain we were . . . married."

The Earl knew what she was trying to explain and he said:

"I think that is a very sensible suggestion, Lynetta, and I am sure we will both sleep well and be very comfortable."

Now she looked at him again and asked:

"You . . . do not think it . . . wrong of me to . . . suggest it?"

"I think it was very kind of you."

"I cannot help thinking," Lynetta went on, "that if we did anything . . . unusual . . . then somehow Ségar might be able to . . . capture me, and even the First Consul would not be able to . . . prevent it."

"I think you are exaggerating Ségar's importance,"

the Earl said, "but I agree with you; having told our story, we must make absolutely certain that everybody believes it."

He was thinking it was very intelligent of Lynetta to have thought of such a solution.

He also realised that she was very young and innocent.

It had obviously never crossed her mind that a man, lying beside her, however much she trusted him, might be a danger in a very different way.

"Get undressed," he said, "and of course you should ring for the maid who will be waiting up for you."

Obediently she moved toward the bellpull, and he smiled as he went through the communicating door.

"I 'ears wot Her Ladyship suggested, an' very sensible I thinks it is too!" Hunt said.

The Earl thought he ought to reprove him for listening at the keyhole, considering Lynetta had been almost whispering. Then he thought it a waste of time.

"The sooner we can get back to the yacht, the better!" he said. "I will see Daguerre first thing in the morning, and arrange for the wagons to collect what we have bought from the Château, and what he has for me. Then we can be on our way."

"Yes, o' course, M'Lord," Hunt said, "'though it seems a pity you can't enjoy a bit of Gay Paree while you're 'ere."

The Earl did not say anything and Hunt went on:

"From all I 'ears, however, Yer Lordship didn't miss much at dinner."

"What do you mean by that?" the Earl enquired.

"Th' General likes very plain food, not th' sort o' dishes Your Lordship enjoys."

The Earl, who was taking off his clothes, did not bother to answer, and Hunt went on:

"Wot he do like, and they was laughin' about it downstairs, is 'ot baths!"

"Hot baths?" the Earl exclaimed.

"'E lies in 'em for at least an hour," Hunt related, "continually turning on the geyser taps and fillin' th' place with steam!"

The Earl thought it rather eccentric, but he did not say so, thinking it a mistake to encourage Hunt, who was an inveterate gossip.

He undressed and put on a long silk robe, which he had recently bought, and he told Hunt to be ready for him at eight o'clock next morning.

When the valet had gone, the Earl walked to the communicating door and knocked softly.

He heard Lynetta call out, "Come . . . in!" and opened the door to find that she was in bed.

She looked very small and insubstantial under the huge gold corona.

She was wearing a very elegant lace-trimmed nightgown that she had acquired from the dressmaker. Her hair was falling over her shoulders as it had done when he had awakened her late in the afternoon.

The Earl walked to the bed and in the light from two candles left burning on the other side he could see her face.

Her eyes were very large, her lips parted.

He sat down on the bed facing her and asked: "What is upsetting you?"

"I . . . I am just . . . afraid that you . . . might be angry with me!"

"Why should you think that?"

"I . . . I knew to-night when we were with all those people upstairs how . . . very important you were . . . and I knew that it would be . . . very difficult for you if it was . . . discovered that . . . you had been . . . lying to them."

"I think it would be better for me to be caught lying than for you to be trapped by a beast like Ségar," the Earl said.

"But . . . that is . . . my problem . . . not yours . . . and you are so kind . . . so very, very kind that it makes me feel . . . guilty."

"I think the truth is," the Earl said, "that you are tired. What you have to do, Lynetta, is to accept things as they come, and try to enjoy yourself."

He took her hand in both of his and felt her fingers quivering.

It was as if he had caught a little bird, and he wanted to put his arms around her and comfort her, as he would a child.

Then he told himself that would make things much worse than they were already.

"I want you to go to sleep," he said aloud, "and tomorrow when you wake up, we can laugh together over the strange adventures we are having, you and I."

"Will you . . . really laugh?" Lynetta asked. "Or will you think I am . . . a horrible woman who is . . . causing you a . . . lot of trouble?"

The Earl laughed. "I promise you I will not think that. Quite frankly, I am enjoying solving a difficult puzzle and thinking I am very clever to find a way out of a maze."

"That is exactly what you have done!" Lynetta said. "Found a way out of a maze from which I . . . believed there was . . . no exit and never . . . would be."

"You were wrong," the Earl said. "And now, Lynetta, as I am also tired, I am going to bed, and I hope you do not snore!"

"Now what makes you think I snore . . . ?" Lynetta began.

Then she realised that once again the Earl was teasing her, and laughed.

"If there is any snoring in here tonight," she said, "it is more likely to be you! Mama always said that men snore because they lie on their backs."

"Then I will lie on my side," the Earl promised.

He released her hand, thinking that since he had held it close in his she had stopped trembling.

Then he walked round the bed, and instead of taking off his robe, he kept it on.

"I asked for an extra blanket," Lynetta said, "and you also have the eiderdown, if you are cold."

"I see you will make somebody a very good wife one of these days," the Earl replied, "and when we get to England, I will find you a really charming husband."

Lynetta did not answer and he had the feeling she did not wish to think of marriage.

"In the meantime," he said as he pulled the blanket over him, and then the eiderdown, "we have a great deal to do in finding your relations, and of course you must tell me where in my house you think your father and mother's furniture will look best."

It struck him as he spoke that that was something Elaine would want to do.

Then he was aware that he had not actually thought about her for some time.

There were so many other things to hold his attention.

"I would love to do that," Lynetta said in a soft voice. "Are you . . . comfortable?"

The Earl found the bed soft; the pillow on which he was lying was of fine linen and smelt of lavender; and it would be impossible for any man to complain.

"I am delighted with our new accommodation," he said. "Shall I blow out the candles?"

"Yes, please," Lynetta answered, "I left them on your side of the bed because I thought that was what you would do."

The candles were extinguished and they were in the dark.

The Earl thought that Henry, as well as a great many of his other friends at White's would not believe it if they could see him.

He was sleeping in the same bed as a very beautiful woman, but was making no effort to touch her.

"Good-night, Lynetta," he said.

"Good-night," she answered. "I am . . . just thanking God with all . . . my heart that you . . . came to the Château . . . and that you . . . saved me."

· She paused for a moment before she added: "I am sure that . . . God sent you and that Papa and Mama are . . . very . . . happy that I am . . . with you."

The Earl thought he had never heard any words so sincerely and movingly spoken.

He shut his eyes and thought that of all the strange situations he had been in his life, this was undoubtedly the strangest!

And perhaps, because it was so unexpected, the most intriguing.

chapter five

It had taken the Earl a long time to get to sleep as he listened to Lynetta's soft breathing.

He awoke early and, slipping out of bed so as not to waken her, he went into his Dressing-room.

He drew back the curtains and looked out at the beauty of the Tuileries Gardens. They had been restored to their past glory since Bonaparte had come to the Palace.

He found it rather extraordinary that one man should have changed the rampaging horror and terror and the disruption of French life, so quickly.

There was no doubt, the Earl thought, whatever his enemies might say of him, that Bonaparte was a great man.

At the same time, he had no wish to stay as his guest for longer than was absolutely necessary.

He decided he would tell Daguerre to send for the furniture from the Château as quickly as possible; then he and Lynetta could be on their way to Calais.

He thought, however, it would make things easier if Daguerre came to him; he knew the Intermediary would be only too pleased to come to the Tuileries.

As soon as Hunt called him he asked to speak to one of the be-gilt officials who appeared to have nothing to do.

When one came to his dressing-room the Earl arranged that he should take his Note of Hand to the Bank.

At the same time, he asked Daguerre to visit him in the Palace immediately.

He was aware that the request would be carried out with military precision and efficiency.

He was not surprised when, later in the morning, he saw the First Consul taking the salute with his troops.

The immense area of the Carousel was crowded with all the pomp and splendour of Royalty.

Riding a horse that had belonged to the late King, Bonaparte passed along the line of his men. With his cropped hair, high nose, and intense searching eyes, he looked every inch a leader.

He was attended by his Generals.

Amidst the glittering throng, he stood out in his black unlaced hat and plain blue uniform.

'He might be an ordinary English sea captain!' the Earl thought with a smile.

But he knew there was nothing ordinary or insignificant about the little man on horseback. In fact Bonaparte made him think of Caesar.

He was sure, and he thought it was what the War Party in England would want to hear, that behind the façade of Roman Republican Reforms, he was intent on Imperial power.

"You will hardly believe," a distinguished Frenchman said to him in a low voice, "that two years ago the country was on the verge of collapse!"

"I agree with you that it is a miracle," the Earl replied.

At the same time he was apprehensive as to what part England was expected to play in the new Europe which Bonaparte was building so swiftly.

When he had a chance of talking to the First Consul, the Earl realised he had the supreme quality of genius and inexhaustible energy.

He learnt that Bonaparte could work for eighteen hours at a stretch and take in the most complicated document at a glance.

But he had an Achilles' Heel, in that like most sensitive leaders of men, he had a very quick temper.

With his iron will, the Earl learned, he was able to keep it in check, but by no means always.

He would flare up if work was badly done by a servant or by one of his Generals.

"More than once on the battlefield," said a French Courtier, with whom the Earl was discussing the First Consul, "Bonaparte lost his temper and struck a General full in the face!"

The Earl collected every detail he could. He knew that it was something those in England should know, especially the Secretary of State for Foreign Affairs.

Lynetta was in the meantime having a very different insight into life in the Palace.

When she was dressing with the aid of two *femmes-de-chambre*, she was told that *Madame* Bonaparte wished to receive her.

She put on one of the pretty gowns she had chosen

the previous day, and was escorted to Josephine Bonaparte's bedroom which was on the same floor as her own.

It was prettily decorated in blue and *Madame* Bonaparte, wearing a very elaborate négligée, was having her hair dressed.

She greeted Lynetta charmingly and when she was sitting beside her said:

"It is exciting to know that you are on your honeymoon! Your husband is extremely handsome!"

"I am very . . . fortunate," Lynetta murmured, feeling this was rather embarrassing.

"My husband has always said," Josephine Bonaparte remarked, "that there is a magnetic fluid between two people who love each other. I am sure that is what you will find."

"I hope . . . so," Lynetta murmured.

"Your gown is delightful!" Josephine remarked, changing the subject.

"It is different from anything I have ever seen before," Lynetta admitted. "My husband bought it for me yesterday because all my luggage was lost."

"Your luggage was lost?" Josephine exclaimed. "What a disaster! At the same time, it is a delight that you can buy everything new."

She became very animated and told Lynetta what were the best shops in which she would find the smartest clothes.

She was obviously anxious to go with her to help her choose them.

Lynetta did not quite know what to do, but she thought is best to agree with anything her hostess suggested.

Living in the country and hidden from everybody,

she had no idea that Napoleon Bonaparte was often outraged by his wife's extravagance.

It was in fact the one point on which he scolded her.

Those who knew Josephine were aware that it went against her soft heart to turn down goods that were submitted to her, however expensive.

It was a weakness on which unscrupulous dressmakers learned to play.

There was a somewhat cynical smile on her hairdresser's face as he listened to what Josephine was saying.

He was thinking of the story that had been circulated all over Paris that when Napoleon was in Egypt, his wife had bought thirty-eight plumed hats at 1,800 francs per hat!

Also her debts at the beginning of the Consulate amounted to 1,200,000 francs.

Lynetta, however, was ignorant of her hostess's besetting sin, and she agreed they should go shopping after luncheon.

Some of the most important *couturiers*, Josephine informed her, had moved into the big houses.

Their owners had either flown the country or been guillotined. She spoke casually, but Lynetta drew in her breath.

For a moment she thought that nothing could make her wear clothes purchased in such surroundings.

Then she knew she must control herself and remember she was English, and not concerned with anything to do with Terror.

Because of her husband's instructions, Josephine Bonaparte was trying to please her English guests. To do so she brought out her jewellery.

One necklace had been made from a set of pearls that had belonged to Marie Antoinette.

"It cost," she said proudly, "250,000 francs!"

Remembering how difficult it had been to find enough money for her and *Mademoiselle* Bernier to eat, Lynetta did not reply.

She wanted to be with the Earl, and feel that he would prevent her from making a mistake.

Luncheon was a fairly simple meal with only twelve guests. The Great Man himself was not present.

Josephine told Lynetta that he ate only two meals a day.

"He has luncheon at eleven," she said, "which he takes alone at a small mahogany pedestal table."

She saw Lynetta was interested, and continued:

"He has dinner at about ten-thirty, which he eats with me and any guests that have been invited."

Madame Bonaparte laughed as she added:

"It is a joke that the Second Consul eats far better meals than we do because my husband dislikes pâté and dishes cooked with cream."

Lynetta thought how much she enjoyed them, and *Madame* Bonaparte went on:

"Napoleon says to our friends: 'If you eat quickly, dine with me. If you eat well, dine with the Second Consul, but if you want to eat badly, do so with the Third!'"

Lynetta thought it very funny. But, when they sat down to luncheon, she realised that, as General Bonaparte was not there, the dishes were cooked with cream.

She found too that the wines were plentiful and delicious.

She had not seen the Earl all the morning and only when she went to wash her hands before luncheon had he come to the bedroom.

"I heard you were with *Madame* Bonaparte," he said.

"I am so glad you have come," Lynetta replied. "She

wants me to go shopping with her, and I do not know how to refuse."

"I think it is a good idea," the Earl said, "I believe she is very extravagant, but I am sure you will not bankrupt me!"

"I would rather be with . . . you."

"I have promised to go with the General to see some of his new armaments," the Earl explained, "and I feel it is something I should do."

He thought, although he did not say so to Lynetta, that it would be important from England's point of view.

Bonaparte was obviously trying to impress him with the strength of the French Army.

"They . . . both seem . . . very friendly," Lynetta said tentatively.

The Earl smiled.

"I am told that Bonaparte now keeps busts of Fox and Nelson on either side of his chimneypiece."

"I am sure that shows he . . . means to keep the peace," Lynetta said.

"I sincerely hope so," the Earl remarked.

When they went their separate ways Lynetta thought wistfully that she wanted to be with him.

She let Josephine persuade her into buying several very elaborate and beautiful gowns. She also chose an evening wrap because she was told they were going to the Opera that evening.

"I think it is something you will enjoy as much as I shall," Josephine said, "and I can only hope my husband will stay to the end."

Lynetta looked surprised, and she explained:

"When we go to the Theatre he has a habit of walking out after the first Act. He says he can guess what is going to happen after that!"

"And what do you do?" Lynetta enquired.

"Sometimes I stay behind. I would rather watch what happens at the end than guess it."

They both laughed as if she had made a joke.

Lynetta wondered if the Earl would enjoy the Opera or be bored by it.

When they got back to the Palace she felt lost because there was no sign of the Earl and she was nervous at being without him.

She went to her bedroom.

It was only when she began to dress for dinner that he came hurrying in.

"Are you all right?" he enquired.

"Yes . . . but where have . . . you been?" Lynetta asked.

"I am up to my eyes in cannon, muskets, and pistols," he answered. "In fact I feel like a barrel of gunpowder which might explode at any moment!"

Before she had time to reply he had gone into his Dressing-room where Hunt had a bath waiting for him.

"You're goin' to the Opera to-night, M'Lord," Hunt informed him.

The Earl groaned.

"A little music goes a long way as far as I am concerned," he said, "especially when I am sitting on a hard seat."

"Your Lordship'll be in the Royal Box all right," Hunt said. "It's all pomp and kissie-the-'and!"

"That is what I thought," the Earl said as he undressed, "and the sooner we leave the better!"

He had seen Daguerre in the morning, who had promised that the wagons would leave for the Château within a few hours of their conversation.

"They will then set off for Calais," the Frenchman said, "and should be there in three days."

The Earl reckoned that, if he and Lynetta left some

104

time the day after to-morrow, they would arrive at about the same time.

He had no wish to linger at the Tuileries knowing that, from Lynetta's point of view, it was dangerous.

He also felt that he knew enough about Napoleon Bonaparte.

He could advise the Prime Minister and anyone else who was interested on what sort of man he was.

When the Earl was dressed he knocked on the communicating door.

When Lynetta told him to come in he found that she was ready, wearing a silver gown which made her look like a streak of moonlight.

Her hair seemed touched with the same light, and her eyes, he thought, were shining like stars.

"You are ready?" he asked somewhat unnecessarily.

"I am so glad you are here," she answered. "I was worried when you were away for so long."

"I told you not to worry!" the Earl replied automatically. "Instead, let me tell you how beautiful you look!"

Lynetta gave a little exclamation of delight and he said:

"I have to apologise to you."

"Apologise?" she asked.

"I meant to buy you some jewellery to-day, and a new wedding ring, but Bonaparte would not let me leave him."

"I missed you," Lynetta said simply.

"Well, the furniture is now on the way," the Earl said, "and that means we can leave on Wednesday."

He knew from the expression on Lynetta's face that was what she wanted to hear.

As they walked side by side up towards the Salon he thought her reliance on him was touching, but rather restricting.

'She will soon find her feet once she gets to London,' he assured himself.

He had the feeling, however, that for some time at any rate, Lynetta would cling to him as her only friend, the only bulwark in a strange and frightening world.

They met the guests who had been invited to go with them to the Opera, who were intelligent, witty, and very sophisticated.

The Earl thought that they must be somewhat frightening for Lynetta.

When a man was being over-effusively complimentary to her he saw that she was upset and went to her rescue.

Fortunately dinner did not consist of many courses.

They set off in a number of comfortable and well-sprung carriages.

Because the Earl was the Guest of Honour, he and Lynetta travelled with the First Consul and *Madame* Bonaparte.

There were soldiers riding before and behind them, and a bodyguard of aides-de-camp and officials escorted them to the Royal Box.

There were more soldiers posted at attention outside it all through the performance.

It was as excellent a production as it would have been in the past when the King and Queen were present.

The Earl, however, was not surprised when, halfway through the First Act, Bonaparte began to fidget, and finally rose to his feet.

He was oblivious to the fact that the performers were still singing on the stage.

The First Consul and his wife, followed by the Earl and Lynetta, left.

They were bowed from the building and once again

escorted by a large bodyguard down the steps to where their carriages were waiting.

Napoleon Bonaparte and his wife entered the carriage first.

As they did so the Earl heard Lynetta give a little gasp of horror, and he felt her hand clutch hold of his.

She was trembling and with a quickness which was characteristic of him he pushed her into the carriage.

He seated himself beside her opposite their host and hostess.

By the light coming through the windows he could see she had gone very pale and he was also aware that there was a look of terror in her large eyes.

He took her hand and held it tightly to give her courage.

Then he started to tell Bonaparte an amusing episode that had taken place at Carlton House.

He was giving Lynetta a chance to get over the shock of whatever had upset her.

Although her fingers still trembled in him, he knew when they reached the Tuileries her feelings were under control.

Fortunately, as Bonaparte was in a hurry to get to bed they did not linger over their good-nights.

Within five minutes of reaching the Palace, the Earl and Lynetta were in their bedroom.

He shut the door and asked:

"What has upset you?"

"It was . . . Jacques Ségar! He was in . . . the street . . . outside the . . . Opera House!"

"I thought it must be something like that!" the Earl exclaimed, "but do you think he recognised you?"

"He was staring . . . straight at me . . . and I am . . . very like . . . Mama."

"You cannot be certain that he thought it was you," the Earl said.

He was trying to be comforting, but he saw the terror was back in Lynetta's eyes.

"Get ready for bed," he said gently. "and we will talk about it later. I can see you are tired and when one is tired everything seems worse."

He knew what he said was poor comfort, and as he walked into the Dressing-room he decided that the sooner they got away the better.

Even if Ségar had not recognised Lynetta, the continual anxiety and fear was like an evil poison.

"Has anything happened to-night, Hunt?" he asked, as he valet helped him out of his evening clothes.

"Nothin' much, M'Lord," Hunt answered. "That English valet be too nosy for my likin', 'though he's a great admirer of Your Lordship."

"Say as little to him as you can," the Earl advised.

"I keeps me mouth shut!" Hunt said.

The Earl went back into the room next door and found Lynetta sitting up in bed and knew she had been waiting for him.

The night was warm. When he had blown out the candles he took off the long robe which he had worn the previous night.

He got into bed in his silk nightshirt, covering himself with only the blanket.

Then, as he lay back against the pillows, he said:

"Now we can talk without being afraid of being overheard."

"Please . . . let us go . . . away!" Lynetta begged. "If we stay here . . . I am sure . . . he will find . . . some way of . . . killing me."

"That would be impossible," the Earl replied, "seeing the number of soldiers there are both in the Palace and outside. If they can protect Bonaparte, they can certainly protect one small and very young woman!"

"I . . . I am . . . frightened!" Lynetta murmured.

"I promise you we will leave as soon as I can arrange it," the Earl said.

"Do you . . . mean . . . that?"

"I always mean what I say. I will think out an excuse to ask Bonaparte for protection during our journey to Calais."

"Yes . . . yes . . . you must do . . . that!" Lynetta cried frantically. "He might be . . . waiting for us . . . on the road . . . and he will . . . carry me away . . . as he did Papa and Mama!"

"I promise you that will not happen," the Earl said quietly. "Now go to sleep, Lynetta, and to-morrow I will make sure I am with you all day."

"That will be . . . wonderful!"

He realised she was trying to be self-controlled.

He admired her because she did not say any more, but turned over on her side as if she intended to go to sleep.

Because he felt unexpectedly tired after listening to Bonaparte's staccato explanatory remarks all day, the Earl shut his eyes.

He must have fallen into a deep sleep.

It was a long time later when he was awakened by Lynetta giving a scream that was like that of an animal caught in a trap.

Then she was saying: "He is . . . taking me . . . away! He is . . . going to . . . kill me! Save . . . me! Save . . . me!"

The Earl realised she had turned towards him and at the same time he was aware that she was dreaming.

He sat up in bed and, as he did so, Lynetta flung herself against him.

He put his arms around her.

"It is all right," he said soothingly. "You have just had a bad dream and you are really quite safe."

She hid her face against his neck and he could feel her hands clutching at his silk nightshirt.

"He . . . was there! . . . I saw him! . . . He was . . . reaching out . . . towards . . . me!"

"You are still dreaming," the Earl said. "Wake up, Lynetta! You are quite safe, I promise you."

It was then that she burst into tears.

It was the culmination, the Earl knew, of the many months she had been a captive in her own home.

He could understand the agony of her knowing that Ségar was waiting for her, and having to hide in the dark passage had at last begun to take its toll.

She was crying uncontrollably and helplessly, like a child.

As he held her close he could feel her tears wet on the fine silk of his nightshirt, and then they percolated through to his bare skin.

He drew her a little closer.

There was the softness and warmth of her body as she trembled against him.

She was still crying, and he knew it was a storm which had been pent up inside her for too long.

"It is all right! It is all over!" he said softly. "When we are in England you will be able to forget that all this has ever happened."

He stroked her hair and found it was as soft and silky as it looked.

He was aware there was a faint fragrance about it; she must have washed it with an essence of violets or perhaps of rose-petals.

Gradually her sobs grew less, but she did not move, and her hands still clutched his nightshirt.

Then at last she was still until she said in a tremulous little voice: "I . . . I am . . . sorry."

"There is no need to be sorry," the Earl said. "I understand it was a shock seeing Ségar."

"I used to . . . peep at him . . . from the . . . windows of the . . . cottage when . . . he walked about the garden . . . but he looked . . . even more . . . frightening to-night."

"I think what you are imagining is worse than it is," the Earl reassured her.

His arms tightened as he said:

"I expect he was really hating Bonaparte, thinking that he has become, with all his pomp and glory, an aristocrat!"

"H-he was . . . looking at m-me!" Lynetta answered.

"Then we must just make sure he does not see you again."

"C-can we do . . . that?"

It was like the question of a child who wanted to be reassured that she was safe.

"You will have to trust me to take care of you," the Earl said quietly.

As he spoke, he knew that it was something he would do even if he died in the attempt.

He wanted to save Lynetta, he wanted to protect her and to comfort her. He wanted, above all else, to make her happy.

He felt his whole being go out towards her in his determination to do so.

Then, as he heard her give a last little sob that was in a way a cry of joy, he knew that he loved her.

He had never felt for any woman what he felt at this moment for Lynetta.

He had been thinking of her as a child that he must

look after, whom he must save from a Dragon in the shape of Ségar.

Now, in his arms, she was a woman, a very lovely and very desirable woman.

What he felt for her was so different from anything he had felt in the past for Elaine, or indeed any of the Beauties who had preceded her.

He felt Lynetta was already a part of himself.

She was incomplete without his protection, and he was incomplete without the feelings she gave him.

She made him believe he was capable of any deed, however difficult, in order to save her from any further suffering.

"I love you!" he wanted to say, but because he loved her he knew perceptively that it would be a mistake.

She had still not for one moment thought of him as a man. She was not shy or embarrassed that their bodies were touching.

Now he could feel the softness of her breasts against his chest and her warmth as his arms encircled her.

He was still the rock to which she clung, a rock which would save her from drowning in a frightening, tempestuous sea.

He knew that to destroy this image before she was ready might make her more afraid than she was.

'I must be very careful not to hurt her,' the Earl thought.

He did not realise then that this was something he had never felt before. In his relations with all other woman he had thought only of himself.

Now he would not even allow his lips to touch Lynetta's hair in case she should be aware of it.

Instead he said in a deliberately calm and gentle voice:

"I want you to lie down again and go back to sleep."

112

She made a little murmur, and he went on:

"We have a great deal to do to-morrow, and you must help me to get away quickly to where the *Sea Lion* is waiting for us."

"To take . . . us to . . . England!" Lynetta said beneath her breath.

"To take you to where you will be free and unafraid for the rest of your life!"

Lynetta drew a deep breath.

Then, for the first time since she had flung herself at him, she raised her head.

"My tears . . . have made . . . you wet!"

"That is no great disaster," the Earl smiled.

He put his arm out above the sheet so that she could slip down into her side of the bed, but for the moment she still clung to him.

"You . . . you will not . . . go away?"

"I will be here beside you."

"You . . . promise?"

"I promise!"

She moved a little further away from him, but then put out her hand to hold onto his.

"If I can . . . touch you," she whispered, "I will not . . . dream such . . . horrible things . . . again."

"If I move a little nearer you will be more comfortable," the Earl said.

He got off the bed, and slipped inside the sheet and blanket that covered Lynetta.

Then he turned towards her so that their hands could meet quite naturally.

"That is . . . better!" she murmured.

She moved a little closer to him and now they were facing each other, their heads on separate pillows.

The Earl knew he had to move only a few inches to reach her lips.

His instinct told him, however, that it was the wrong moment to do so, and it might be a momentous mistake which would sweep away her sense of security.

He wanted her and felt the blood throbbing in his temples, his whole body pulsating with his need to kiss her.

He wanted to hold her close and make love to her.

Setting his own feelings aside, he forced himself to think only of her.

"Go to sleep, Lynetta," he said. "You know I am here, and I promise you I will not go away."

Her fingers tightened on his.

"Good-night," she said. "Thank you for . . . being so . . . very . . . very . . . wonderful!"

Her voice sounded sleepy as she murmured again:

"So . . . very . . . wonderful . . ."

The Earl realised she was asleep, worn out with emotions that had been violent and traumatic, but completely understandable.

Her fingers loosened their grip on his, but she was still touching him.

He had the feeling that if he took his hand away she would wake up.

He lay listening to her breathing.

He was aware that perhaps for the first time in his life he was thinking only of the person he loved.

Then he thought of Elaine, and her name was written in letters of fire in the darkness of the room.

He knew she constituted a danger to his happiness that he had never envisaged.

What he had felt for her was not love, but physical desire because she was so beautiful.

Secondly, to win her would proclaim his superiority over all her other suitors, especially the Marquess of Hampton.

"How can I have been such a fool?" the Earl asked himself.

Then an icy hand was pressed against his forehead.

He remembered the letter he had written to Elaine before he left London. It was a proposal of marriage.

If she accepted, it was as binding as if they had actually exchanged vows in front of an altar.

It was inconceivable that any Gentleman should jilt a woman to whom he was betrothed.

For the Earl to do so, he knew, would be to cause a scandal.

It would involve Elaine's whole family, the head of which was her Grandfather, the Duke of Avondale.

Then there were his relations, a great number of whom held positions at Court.

His behaviour would be condemned by the King and Queen.

The Prince of Wales and everybody who considered themselves of importance in the *Beau Ton*, would be horrified.

The Earl asked himself how he could ever have been so misguided as to have thought Elaine was the person he wanted as a wife.

He knew now that he did not feel in any way for her as he felt for Lynetta.

Elaine was different from other women—he did not deny that.

But he had always had the feeling that beneath her undeniable grace there was something not entirely right.

Because he had been mystified by her indifference and the manner in which she eluded him, it had increased her attraction.

Yet it was something deeper than that to which he could not put a name.

Now he admitted she had just been a challenge—a

prize that he had wanted to win because a number of his contemporaries were also competing for it.

What he felt for Lynetta was different.

She needed him.

He knew that because she was so helpless without him, he could no more leave her than hurt an animal, or be deliberately cruel to a small child.

He had so much, and she had nothing.

He had to make her aware that his love would compensate her for everything she had lost.

But . . . there was Elaine!

In the darkness, with Lynetta holding onto his hand, her body soft, warm, lying within a few inches of his, the Earl went down into Hell.

It was an agony he had never thought or visualised would be waiting for him.

chapter six

THE next morning the Earl had a plan worked out in his
mind.

He went first to see Colonel Réal, who was in charge
of security at the Palace.

The Colonel rose as he entered his office and the Earl
said:

"I have come for your help, Colonel."

"You know I will do anything in my power," Colonel
Réal replied.

The Earl sat down and said:

"When I came here I deliberately did not bring my
wife's jewellery but left it behind in my yacht. As I had
no outriders, I thought it would be a mistake to travel in
a manner which would undoubtedly encourage thieves."

"I agree with you," the Colonel said. "We have had
trouble on the road from Calais already."

"What I have decided," the Earl went on, "is to buy my wife before we leave Paris some of your magnificent jewellery, which I know she admired on *Madame* Bonaparte."

"Certainly some of the best jewellers have opened their shops since the General became the First Consul," the Colonel said, "and I will give you the names of those who are considered the best."

"That would be very kind," the Earl said, "and could I ask you for two things?"

The Colonel looked up and the Earl said:

"First, that I may have an escort when I take my wife to choose the jewellery."

"Of course," the Colonel replied.

"Secondly," the Earl continued, "could we also have one when we leave here for Calais, which I would like to do tomorrow morning?"

The Colonel appeared to think this was quite a reasonable request. The Earl then went to find Lynetta, who was getting dressed.

He realised when he entered the bedroom that she was looking exceedingly lovely in a new gown, which she had bought when she had been shopping with *Madame* Bonaparte.

"I heard you had gone out," she said, and he realised it had made her nervous.

"I only went to see Colonel Réal," the Earl replied, "and I will tell you about it later."

"I shall be ready in a few minutes," Lynetta said. "Are we staying in the Palace?"

The Earl knew she was frightened of leaving what she thought of as the security of the Tuileries.

When the maid who was helping her dress had left the room he replied:

"We are going shopping, but set your mind at rest. We have an escort."

Lynetta laughed.

"We are getting very grand!"

"And quite rightly so," the Earl said. "Who could be more important than you?"

She laughed as if it was a very good joke. The Earl thought that to him she was more important than anybody he had ever known.

He wondered how soon he would be able to tell her so. He knew, however, he must be very careful not to upset her.

Then, a few minutes later, as they were leaving her bedroom, she quite unselfconsciously slipped her hand into his.

He was aware, and it was a sobering thought, that she was thinking of him as if he was her father.

The carriage was waiting for them.

There were two soldiers to ride on each side of it as they swept out of the Palace gardens into the busy street.

The coachman had his instructions from Colonel Réal and he took them to an impressive-looking jeweller's shop which was in the Rue du Faubourg St. Honore.

On the way the Earl explained to Lynetta that he was giving her a present,

"Oh, no!" she exclaimed. "You must . . . not do that! You have spent so much . . . money already . . . on my clothes!"

"I not only want to give you something because you will enjoy it," he said quietly, "but it is also part of the plan which I know will get us to the yacht in safety."

She looked at him with wide eyes and he explained:

"We are leaving to-morrow and Colonel Réal has

promised us an escort all the way to Calais."

Lynetta clasped her hands together with delight.

As she did so the Earl realised that she moved a little closer to him as if already she was afraid that somehow she might be snatched away from him on the journey.

As they had come from the Tuileries, they were bowed into the jeweller's shop as if they were Royalty.

The Earl guessed that some of the expensive and magnificent jewels that *Madame* Bonaparte possessed had been bought from this particular establishment.

There was an excellent display, and Lynetta was entranced.

There were jewels of the eighteenth century and some of them were diamond bouquets and foliage, which had been remarkable at the time.

Lynetta was staring at a spray of eglantine and lilies-of-the-valley and the Earl had moved away to admire some necklaces when a woman came into the shop.

She was very elegantly dressed and for the moment she just stood looking around her.

Then she gave a cry of delight when she saw the Earl.

"Darrill!" she exclaimed with pleasure. "Is it really you?"

The Earl turned around and smiled.

"Marguerite!" he said. "I was not expecting to see you here!"

"I have only just arrived," she said, "and if you are to be in Paris when I am, I can imagine nothing more wonderful!"

As she spoke she was clinging onto the Earl's hand with both of hers.

Lynetta thought, with her face turned up to his and with her lips parted provocatively, that she was the most attractive woman she had ever seen.

"You have not told me what you are doing in Paris," the Earl said.

"I am giving a performance at the *Théâtre des Variétés*," she replied, "and hoping of course I can entice Napoleon Bonaparte to be there."

"I am sure you will," the Earl answered, "and you are looking very beautiful, Marguerite."

"That is what I want you to say," she answered, "and tell me, my handsome and most exciting lover, when I can see you?"

She spoke the last words in a low voice. She was thinking that as she was speaking in English it would not be indiscreet in front of the French staff.

Lynetta, however, had heard every word and now she turned away to stare at the jewels in front of her with unseeing eyes.

For the first time she was aware that the Earl was a very attractive man who had made love to the beautiful woman who was standing so close to him!

What that entailed she had no idea, but it had taken her by surprise.

Because she had been so terrified of Jacques Ségar, she had thought of the Earl as a Knight in Armour, who had saved her from the Dragon.

Or perhaps as the Archangel Michael!

He had swept down from the skies to carry her away from the darkness of the passage where she had hidden for so long.

When the Earl had taken her to the Tuileries she had been frightened by the compliments paid her by the Frenchmen, and also by the way they looked at her.

She wanted only to be close to the Earl and know that he protected her from them.

It had never entered her mind that she might need

protection from him! She had also not thought of him as a man who considered her as a woman.

Marguerite, whoever she might be, was now whispering to the Earl and making him laugh.

Lynetta wanted to put her hands over her ears in case she overheard what she was saying.

It had never struck her before how bored the Earl must be with her! Yet he had stayed with her when he could have enjoyed himself with and be amused by lovely women like Marguerite.

"I have not amused him," Lynetta told herself. "All I have done is to cry on his shoulder, and be a nuisance."

She felt suddenly depressed, as if she was covered by a dark cloud that had enveloped her unexpectedly.

She did not understand her own feelings. She only knew that every second while Marguerite was laughing with the Earl, it was as if a thousand little daggers were piercing her heart.

She felt both shy and insignificant, but was not certain what she should do about it.

Finally she heard the Earl say:

"I am leaving to-morrow, Marguerite, and as I cannot see you on this visit, I shall return to Paris very shortly."

"You promise? You promise you will do that? Is there not just a few minutes that we might be together before you go?"

"I am afraid not," the Earl replied. "And I know, Marguerite, you will be a great success. I promise you I will tell the First Consul to come and see your performance."

"That would be very helpful," Marguerite said. "Thank you, darling Darrill!"

As she finished speaking she put her arms around his neck and pulled his head down to hers.

As she kissed him Lynetta gave a little gasp, and

moved to the other end of the shop, as far away as she could.

"How can any woman behave in such an outrageous manner in public?" she asked herself. "And how could the Earl allow it?"

She was holding onto the front of one of the show-cases, as if in need of support.

Then she heard the jeweller saying in French: "Your ear-ring has been repaired, *Mademoiselle*, and I hope it will give you no further trouble."

"*Merci beaucoup!*"

Marguerite spoke with a strong English accent.

Then Lynetta was aware that she was moving to-wards the door.

"*Au revoir*, My Lord," she said as she reached it, "and mind it is *au revoir*, and not good-bye!"

Then she was gone, and Lynetta felt she wanted to cry from sheer relief.

Unaware that she was in any way upset, the Earl was paying attention to the jeweller, who had been fetching his finest jewels from the safe.

He set down a number of leather and velvet boxes on a table. As he walked towards him, the Earl looked round, and seeing Lynetta, said: "Come and look at these, and tell me which you prefer."

In answer Lynetta wanted to say that she would have none of them.

Then she realised the Earl would not understand and just think she was being ungrateful.

With a tremendous effort at self-control, she forced herself to walk slowly towards him, and the vendeur hurried to place a chair for her in front of the table.

First the Earl asked for wedding rings. There was a big choice but they found one which fitted Lynetta.

It was plain gold and unusually narrow.

"Do you like it?" the Earl asked.

"Yes, thank you."

Lynetta told herself it was all part of the act. He did not care what she felt about a ring which would be thrown away when they reached England.

The Earl was looking at a magnificent necklace fashioned like stars. There was another which was of jewelled lilac blossom, a triumph of an eighteenth century craftsman's art.

A necklace fashioned with sapphires was not so impressive as one of rubies, and a third was of turquoises surrounded with diamonds.

The Earl inspected them all but Lynetta sat beside him and said nothing.

All she could think of was the fascination of Marguerite's face, and the way she had kissed the Earl.

She found herself wondering what she would feel if he kissed her.

Although he was not aware of it, she looked at his lips from under her eye-lashes, and felt a strange sensation within her breasts. It was something she had never known before.

Then the Earl was asking her a question.

"Which do you think the most attractive, Lynne?" he enquired.

"I . . . I do not . . . know."

She thought as she spoke that she sounded stupid, and with an effort she added:

"The star necklace is very beautiful!"

The Earl thought they were like her eyes and he said: "Put it on, and let me see if it becomes you."

It was fashionable even for a day-gown to be made low in the neck.

Lynetta had covered herself when she left the Tuileries with a wrap of velvet in the same colour as her muslin gown.

Now she slipped it off from her shoulders and one of the vendeurs clasped the diamond star necklace round her neck.

The stars had been graded from very small ones at the back to a large one at the front.

The Earl thought that against her white skin it looked very alluring.

He realised that Lynetta's long neck was enhanced by the jewels, and he found himself wondering what she would look like if she wore them and nothing else.

Just for a moment his desire for her seemed to rise up within him like a tidal wave.

Then with an effort he forced himself to look away and say almost sharply:

"Try on the turquoises."

He thought that around Lynetta's neck they were beautiful, but too hard a contrast to the whiteness of her skin.

The jeweller opened another box. In it was a set which made Lynetta draw in her breath.

Again it had been made in the eighteenth century.

The craftsman had copied the delicacy of wild flowers and incorporated them in a necklace which looked as if it had been fashioned by the fairies.

There were tiny blossoms of forget-me-nots, buttercups and daisies, primroses and wild orchids.

They were all clustered together in a necklace which the Earl thought expressed Lynetta's youth and purity.

There were small, round ear-rings to go with the necklace, besides two bracelets, a brooch, and a ring.

"I was keeping this, *Monsieur*," the jeweller said, "to show to *Madame* Bonaparte."

The Earl did not say they were far more suitable for

Lynetta, he merely answered, "I will take them!"

There was a gleam of delight in the jeweller's eyes, and he named a sum that was so astronomical that Lynetta expected the Earl to say it was too much.

He was actually thinking that it was a very large sum to expend on a present. Yet it would certainly ensure that they had a suitable guard to convey them to Calais.

Also, the Earl thought with the practical part of his mind, although it might be a cost of twelve, perhaps fifteen horses, it would be far more expensive in England.

Only when they were driving back to the Tuileries did Lynetta ask:

"I think the jewel set is exquisite, but what will you do with it when you get home?"

"It is a present for you," the Earl replied.

"But . . . only while we . . . are in . . . France."

He shook his head. "No, it is for you."

She stared at him as if he could not believe what he was saying.

Then as she saw the smile on his lips she said:

"You are . . . teasing me . . . of course . . . you are!"

"It is always a mistake to tease women about themselves," the Earl said. "It is a subject on which they have very little sense of humour!"

"I think that is unfair," Lynetta objected, "and my question is serious. I know you have spent all that money so that we can be guarded until we escape from France, but it is too much!"

"Nothing is too much if it will save you from your enemies!" the Earl replied.

"You are so kind . . . and so clever," Lynetta said, "but you can . . . sell the jewellery when we . . . reach London."

"You still do not understand what I am saying," the

Earl insisted. "It is a present for you, Lynetta, and something which I hope will make you think of the time we have been together."

She stared at him before she said:

"You . . . you . . . really . . . mean that?"

"I invariably mean what I say," the Earl answered, "and I wanted you to have something that would please you."

Lynetta gave a little cry.

"What . . . can I . . . say? How . . . can I . . . thank you?"

"By looking happy," the Earl answered, "and not being afraid."

"You have . . . given me . . . too much," Lynetta murmured, "and I have . . . nothing to . . . give you . . . in return."

The Earl thought he had an answer to that.

At that moment the horses turned into Tuileries Gardens, and he merely remarked:

"You can thank me when we reach the Sea *Lion* and set sail for Dover."

*   *   *

When Lynetta was alone in her room preparing for luncheon, she stared at herself in the mirror.

It was not her own face she saw there, however. It was the face of the fascinating Marguerite with her crimson lips and long dark eyelashes.

Lynetta did not realise that they were made up with mascara.

She wanted to ask the Earl about her and how he came to know her.

But he had said nothing and she felt shy about asking him any questions.

Even as she stared at the mirror she could hear Marguerite's voice saying:

"My handsome and most exciting lover..."

She gasped as if a knife was piercing her heart and it was so painful that she wanted to cry out that she was in agony.

"Why did I not think of him as a man," she asked herself, "and, like all men, enamoured of a beautiful woman?"

Now she could see that the guests who had been entertained at the Tuileries since they had been there were flirting as they sat together at dinner and in the Salon.

The women were very attractive as they looked at the men with shining eyes and with what seemed to Lynetta an invitation on their lips.

"How could I look like that?" she asked, and doubted whether the Earl would notice her.

He kissed Marguerite, or rather, she had kissed him. Once again Lynetta was wondering what it would feel like if he kissed her.

"It is something that will never happen," she told herself.

As she turned from the mirror she saw the bed and remembered how last night, after she had cried, he had lain beside her and she had held his hand.

He had also held her close against him but she had hardly been aware of the strength of his arms or that their bodies were touching.

"How could I have cried in such circumstances? Instead..." she began to ask herself, then stopped.

She could not believe what she was feeling now.

She could not understand why it was agony to think of him kissing Marguerite or the inexpressible joy she had felt because he had said he could not see her while she was in Paris.

"We must go away to-morrow," she decided. "There is nothing to stop us."

She was not thinking, as she had before, of Ségar. There was another enemy, and it was a woman called Marguerite.

During the afternoon the Earl received *Monsieur* Daguerre, who arrived with the final bill for the furniture he had bought.

Listed was not only what he had purchased from the Château de Marigny.

There were six magnificent pieces of Boulle craftsmanship to which the Earl had given only a perfunctory glance because he had been in a hurry.

Daguerre had also discovered for him an absolute treasure.

It was a cabinet made in 1670 and which he assured the Earl was "*la toilette de Madame Maintenon,*" her wash basin.

The panels were *petra pura* and carved figures represented the Four Seasons.

Because he was prepared to trust Daguerre, the Earl accepted what he said. He bargained a little over the price, then wrote him a cheque for the whole amount.

He realised that in any case he had little choice, as Daguerre with a certain cunning had already put everything on the road to Calais.

The whole bill came to quite a considerable sum, but the Earl knew it was worth it and he would undoubtedly provide Charn with a treasure trove it had never possessed before.

Then he remembered he owed the idea to Elaine, and his expression darkened.

Once again the question was back in his mind—what was he to do about her?

That evening the Earl insisted they dine quietly at the Palace no matter what anybody else was doing.

He intended to leave early in the morning, and did not wish, as he told Josephine, for his wife to be over-tired.

It was a decision which pleased Bonaparte and as the dinner-party consisted of only eight persons, the Earl realised it was his last chance of getting to know the First Consul.

Up to now, to the English, Bonaparte had been the Bogey-Man.

Now the Earl had the feeling that they would resent his supremacy over Europe.

He knew that the War Party in Parliament would be watching to prevent any extension of what Napoleon was already thinking of as his Empire.

For the moment, at any rate, Bonaparte was de-lighted with the Peace.

He had attended a solemn *Te Deum* in Notre Dame and spoke of 'the great European family.'

The Earl knew the British reaction to that!

At eleven o'clock, as the Earl expected, Bonaparte was ready for bed.

The guests disappeared, and Josephine, with her arm through Lynetta's, led the way down to their bedrooms.

"You must come and stay with us again, my dear Countess," she said to Lynetta, "and I am sure when we are more established, we shall be able to entertain you better than we have this time."

"You have been kindness itself!" Lynetta protested.

"You are very lovely," Josephine said, "but hold on tightly to your husband! He is far too handsome for most women's peace of mind!"

She kissed Lynetta good-night, and they went to their separate bedrooms.

As she was undressing, Lynetta could still hear her words ringing in her ears.

Of course the Earl was handsome, the most handsome man she had ever seen. Josephine Bonaparte was not the only woman who thought so!

There was Marguerite whom he had kissed, and it was obviously not for the first time.

"There must have been dozens of other women!" she told herself.

The idea of it made her want to cry.

She got into bed, and as she did so she realised that the Earl had not yet come to his Dressing-room.

She could hear Hunt moving about as he waited for him, and it struck her that perhaps he had lingered behind to tell Bonaparte about Marguerite.

Then a different thought struck her.

Perhaps, because it was still early by some people's standards, he had gone to see her.

She wanted to cry out then, not only because he had left her alone, but because of where he had gone.

She waited, straining her ears, longing as she had never longed for anything in her whole life to hear his voice next door.

Then when he did come, and she heard him, she knew why she was so unhappy.

She loved him.

*　　*　　*

Before the Earl came to bed, he had gone to check the arrangements for the morning with Colonel Réal.

He was hoping they could get to Calais in record time.

They had to wait for the furniture, and he thought it

would be better and safer to do so in the yacht. If there was any trouble they could move out to sea.

He thought with satisfaction that he had planned everything very carefully and it would only be extremely bad luck if everything did not take place smoothly and without upsetting Lynetta.

"Have you got everything packed, Hunt?" he asked.

"Everything, includin' 'er Ladyship's trunks, and there's quite a bit more than we 'ad when we arrived."

The Earl smiled.

"That is true."

He had asked for the leather case.

It contained the precious jewellery that he had bought as a present for Lynetta.

He thought it was unusual that she had been so surprised that he should give her a present, and also worried about his extravagance.

He remembered the different presents he had given other women.

The recipients, including Marguerite, had accepted everything he had to give as their right.

Marguerite was actually very different from ordinary actresses or theatrical performers.

The Earl had been her lover for a short time. Yet he had not broken his rule of never paying in cash for a woman's favours.

However, they accepted jewels as they accepted fans and gloves.

He had often thought that there was really little difference in that particular between Ladies and Harlots.

He had not thought it necessary to explain to Lynetta that Marguerite was the daughter of an impoverished Clergyman and had an exquisitely beautiful soprano voice.

She had been discovered when she had sung in

Church. A Peer, who was financing a play that was being produced at one of the playhouses in Bath, heard her.

Very persuasively he enticed her to London and she had become an instant success.

Her father, who was elderly and very poor, had been grateful for the money she had been able to send him.

He had no idea that not all of it came from what she earned on the stage.

She had fallen in love with the Earl and, while he was intrigued to find a lady in such a position, she had asked him:

"Why should I be poor and respectable when I can be rich and command the admiration of Gentlemen like you?"

He had laughed and when finally their liaison, which was never very serious, came to an end, he had given her an expensive diamond brooch.

It never struck him that Lynetta, whom he thought did not think of him as a man, would have been upset by the way Marguerite behaved.

When he went into the bedroom he found that it was in darkness, except for one candle burning on his side of the bed.

Her eyes were closed and he thought she was asleep and it was, in a way, a relief.

It had been an unbearable temptation last night when he was so close to her not to give way to his impulses.

He wanted to kiss her, to hold her, and more than anything else, to make love to her.

Surprisingly, he was suddenly shocked at himself.

He had never in his life seduced a young girl, and one who was of the same class as himself.

Very gently, he lowered himself on top of the bed,

keeping on his long robe as he had the first night, and covered himself with the blanket.

As he fell asleep, he was wondering as he had last night what he should do about Elaine.

Only when he was free of her could he tell Lynetta of his love.

* * *

The Earl and Lynetta set off very early the next morning.

There was only Colonel Réal to usher them into their carriage and bid them bon voyage.

The carriage which had been provided for them by Bonaparte was very much bigger than the one the Earl had bought at Calais.

He had told Daguerre to sell it on his behalf.

He was also pleased with the horses and he learnt that others had been sent ahead the previous morning after he had spoken to the Colonel.

This meant they would be able to change his own every night for the more excellent horseflesh which belonged to the First Consul.

Ready to ride ahead and behind them was a troop of six mounted soldiers and the Earl learned that others had gone ahead to stand guard during the night.

"I cannot thank you enough for all you have done for us, Colonel," he said as he shook hands with him.

Lynetta also thanked him in a gentle voice.

The Earl was aware of the admiration in the Colonel's eyes when he looked at her.

Then they were off.

The sentries on the Palace steps presented arms, and the Colonel raised his hand in salute.

As they drove out of the gardens Lynetta gave a little laugh.

"We are very grand!"

"And very safe!" the Earl added.

"How can you have been so clever as to persuade General Bonaparte that we should be looked after so adequately on our journey?"

"I was thinking of you," the Earl answered, "and I was determined that you should enjoy yourself and not be worried as you have been ever since I have known you."

To his surprise, Lynetta did not smile. Instead she merely looked ahead and said:

"I . . . I realise what a . . . nuisance I have . . . been!"

"Now you are fishing for compliments," the Earl replied. "I enjoy having you with me, Lynetta. In fact, I think it is the most delightful thing that ever happened that *Mademoiselle* Bernier should have brought you to me."

He saw the colour come into Lynetta's cheeks.

But she did not look at him eagerly with the almost childlike delight as she had done before.

Instead she said in a very small voice:

"I . . . I wish that was . . . true."

"Unless you are calling me a liar," the Earl said, "your wish is granted."

Lynetta drew in her breath.

Then, because he did not want to upset her in any way, he pointed out several buildings of interest as they passed through the crowded streets and were finally outside the City and in the countryside.

The horses were swift-footed and the carriage in which they were travelling was comfortable.

There was something reassuring, the Earl thought, in the sound of horses' hooves, with the two soldiers ahead of them and the other four behind.

He seated himself in a corner of the carriage and put up his feet on the small seat opposite.

"We have a long way to go," he said, "so I suggest you take off your bonnet."

Lynetta obeyed him and put it down on the floor.

She had no idea as she did so that the Earl was watching her and thinking that her hair, which had been arranged by Josephine Bonaparte's hairdresser, was very becoming.

He was also remembering how he had touched it when she had cried on his shoulder. It had felt like silk beneath his fingers, and he longed to stroke it again.

The same question sprang back into his mind.

It seemed as if the wheels beneath him were saying over and over again:

"What about Elaine? What about Elaine?"

They stopped for luncheon.

Hunt had brought the dishes from the kitchen at the Tuileries.

There was a bottle of excellent Champagne and delicious pâté and when they drove on again the Earl could not help feeling that even Royalty could not be more comfortable.

Lynetta was very quiet.

At luncheon she had been animated as she listened to everything he said.

Because she was so lovely and he wanted to kiss her, he found himself breaking off in mid-sentence, then having no idea what he had been talking about.

They were out in the matchless countryside, on a narrow, isolated road.

There were trees on either side which almost met overhead and the horses suddenly slowed down.

The Earl looked out of the window.

Then, as the soldiers behind came galloping past, he stood up to see what was happening.

"What . . . is it?" Lynetta asked in a frightened voice.

Even as she spoke there was the sound of gunfire. The horses must have reared and the carriage moved backwards and forwards.

The Earl sat down again.

"It is an . . . ambush!" Lynetta cried. "Ségar is trying to . . . take me! It is . . . Ségar! I know . . . it is!"

The terror was back in her voice and she clung to the Earl frantically.

He put his arms around her.

Now there was more gunfire and it was impossible for him to speak above the noise.

He could feel her trembling violently against him.

He could only pray that it was not what she feared, but if it was the soldiers should be able to protect them.

Then as the carriage came to a standstill, he thought the driver must have got the animals under control, and there was no more gunfire.

The door was suddenly flung open.

It was Hunt! The Earl, holding Lynetta closely against him asked: "What has happened?"

"It was that man Ségar, M'Lord, lurkin' in th' bushes," Hunt said. "'E was with a bunch of villains like hisself!"

Lynetta gave a cry of horror.

"It's all right, M'Lady," Hunt said reassuringly. "'E's dead. Dead as a door-nail, and half-a-dozen rogues wiv 'im!"

Very gently the Earl moved Lynetta away from him.

She tried to protest but he got out of the carriage, saying to Hunt as he did so:

"Look after Her Ladyship."

He emerged to find that the men had chosen a clever place for an ambush.

There were some bushes beneath the trees in which they could hide.

The Sergeant in charge of the soldiers explained to him volubly how the attackers had started to fire too soon and their bullets went wide.

His men had shot Ségar before he could damage anybody or the horses.

The men on the opposite side of the road had fired their muskets without taking proper aim.

The soldiers in front of the carriage had killed two of them and those bringing up the rear had killed three more and wounded two of the others.

The rest had run away.

There was blood everywhere.

Dead bodies were spread across the road. The horses were still restless and sweating.

The Earl, looking down at the dead men, knew that because of his foresight in asking for an escort, they had had a lucky escape.

If nothing else, the expression on Ségar's face told him how brutal his vengeance on Lynetta might have been.

"The sooner we can move on, the better!" he said to the Sergeant.

"That's just what I was going to suggest, *Monsieur*."

"Please thank your men," the Earl said. "I am very grateful to them, and thank God you were here!"

The Sergeant repeated to his men what the Earl had said.

The two soldiers who had been in front saluted with grins on their faces.

The Earl got back into the carriage and, ignoring the

whines and cries of the two wounded men, they drove off.

The Earl was glad for Lynetta's sake that they only had about five miles more to go to where they would stay the night.

When he sat down once again beside her he said very quietly:

"It is all over! Now you are free of Ségar and any other enemies you might have."

"You are . . . you are . . . sure he is . . . dead?"

"Quite sure!" the Earl replied positively. "So smile, Lynetta, because I want you to look happy."

She looked up at him, and there were tears in her eyes.

Then because he was so relieved, so thankful he had not been foolish enough to travel without an escort, he bent towards her.

Without thinking, because he was so utterly relieved that she was unhurt, his lips took possession of hers.

Just for a moment she was still with surprise.

Then as he drew her closer she felt a rapture replace the agony that had been in her breast all night.

He kissed her until she felt that everything had vanished—the coach, the world outside, and the sky.

There was only the Earl.

Because he seemed to take her heart from between her lips and make it his, as he raised his head she said incoherently:

"I . . . I love you . . . I love . . . you!"

"As I love you," the Earl answered.

Then he was kissing her again, kissing her until it was impossible to think, but only to feel.

chapter seven

It took only an hour to reach the place where they were to stay the night, a pleasant *estaminet* set back off the road.

The soldiers who were to guard them at night had already engaged their rooms.

When they went upstairs to change, the Earl found that what was intended as his Dressing-room also contained a bed.

He knew that to-night it would be impossible for him to lie close to Lynetta and not kiss her.

However, he was not prepared, because she was aware of his love for her to be different.

When Lynetta came downstairs to the private Sitting Room where they were to dine, she had changed her gown, rearranged her hair, and looked, the Earl thought, entrancingly lovely.

The moment she came into the room he was aware that she was very shy.

She did not look at him and after a few minutes he said: "To-night we must celebrate, for we have killed the Dragon and now the Princess is free!"

She gave a little laugh, and the colour came and went in her cheeks.

"You . . . killed . . . him," she said softly.

It was with the greatest difficulty that the Earl did not sweep her into his arms as he wanted to do.

He knew, however, the servants would be bringing them dinner, and he did not want to embarrass her in any way.

A servant opened the Champagne.

Then as usual, supervised by Hunt, they were served with what was an excellent meal.

As he wanted Lynetta to feel at ease, the Earl talked of the furniture he had bought, and because he was very knowledgeable, he told her some of the life stories of the craftsmen who had made it.

He was not surprised to find that she knew a great deal, too. Especially about those like Riesener who had worked in the reign of Louis XIV.

"Papa thought he was the greatest craftsman of them all," she said, "although some people prefer André Boulle."

"We have some splendid examples of them both," the Earl said.

"I am longing to see them in . . . your house," Lynetta said, "if ever you should . . . invite me to . . . visit you."

There was an expression in her eyes which told the Earl it was the zenith of her ambition.

He wanted to tell her that his house was hers and it would be their home when they were together.

He knew it was something he dare not say while the thought of Elaine hung over him like the Sword of Damocles.

As soon as dinner was finished they went upstairs to bed and he was aware that, because Lynetta was thinking of him as a man, she was afraid that he would suggest that he sleep beside her.

For the first time she would realise it was wrong, and that it was something she could not allow.

At the same time, she would be aware that if he had not been there she would have been even more terrified.

She had not forgotten her terrible dream that Ségar was trying to capture her.

She knew now it had been prophetic. At the same time, she had not dreamt of the happy ending.

"I am next door," the Earl said, "if you should want me, Lynetta. But you know there is now nothing to frighten you."

"The . . . soldiers are . . . outside?"

"I have told Hunt to speak to them," the Earl said, "and I know that one will be on duty outside your window."

"Then I am . . . sure I shall not . . . disturb you."

The Earl took her hand in his and kissed it. As his lips touched her skin he felt a little quiver run through her.

Then because he could not help himself he turned it over and kissed her palm.

Now her breath came a little quicker through her parted lips.

It was only with a tremendous effort at self-control that the Earl managed to say:

"Good-night, Lynetta, sleep well! We will leave early in the morning."

"Good-night . . . and . . . God   bless . . . you,"   she whispered.

Her door shut and the Earl went to his own room to find Hunt waiting.

"That man won't trouble 'er Ladyship no longer!" Hunt said with relish as he helped the Earl out of his coat.

Because they were still in France he continued to refer to Lynetta as 'Her Ladyship' as the Earl had told him to do.

"If we had not had an escort," the Earl remarked, "things might have been very different."

"They always sez, M'Lord, on the racecourse your Lordship's got the luck o' the devil!"

"I hope you are right," the Earl murmured, but there was a frown above his eyes.

*　　*　　*

The next day they made good progress and there were no unfortunate incidents on the way.

The inn where they stayed was very much the same as that of the night before, but Lynetta was very tired.

The Earl realised that the years when she had been shut up without enough exercise and fresh air were as much responsible for her weakened condition as her lack of food.

She had been content during the day to lie back in the carriage. She held his hand but for most of the time her eyes were shut.

He was not certain whether she was asleep or awake.

Only to look at her made him feel his love for her increasing hour by hour.

He knew it was not only because she was so beautiful. She vibrated to him in a way no other woman had ever done before.

144

He was aware, too, that there was some spiritual bond between them; perhaps the 'magnetic fluid' of which Napoleon had spoken.

Whatever it was, it was a love that was greater and more overwhelming than he had ever imagined it could be.

Because she was so inexperienced with men, Lynetta was quite content just to know he was there and she did not expect him to talk.

The Earl remembered other coach-rides in the past. He had been expected to express his admiration for his companion ceaselessly.

He could remember once saying to Henry:

"Do women ever think of anything else but love?"

"Not when they are with you," Henry had replied.

Now he talked to Lynetta about some building they passed or reminisced about his previous experience in Europe. She not only listened, but also asked him intelligent questions.

Only when their eyes met did he realise that if his body was pulsating with love, so was hers.

'What am I to do?' he asked himself that night in the darkness, as he had asked every night, and had no answer.

Because he loved Lynetta with an adoration that he had never had for anybody else, he could not tell her of his predicament.

It was a problem he had to work out for himself.

Yet, when they were within only a few miles of Calais, he was still in a despair that grew deeper as England drew nearer.

How could he lose Lynetta? She was the other half of himself.

How could he hurt and distress her by leaving her alone in a world of which she knew nothing?

On the other hand, how could he face social ostracism?

That was what it would amount to if he besmirched his family name, and behaved like a cad instead of a gentleman.

When they had their first glimpse of the sea in the distance, Lynetta, who had been very quiet, sat up.

"Are we really nearly there?" she asked.

"Only another mile," the Earl replied.

He turned to look at her eyes, which were shining.

"You have . . . done it! You have . . . done it!" she cried. "How could any man be so . . . wonderful?"

"We have been very lucky."

"God heard . . . my prayers," Lynetta said simply, "and I am sure Papa and Mama were . . . helping us . . . too."

"I am sure they were!" the Earl agreed.

If he had not been almost inspired to ask for an armed guard to escort them to Calais, their story might have been very different.

"You are quite certain . . . your yacht will be . . . there?" Lynetta was asking.

"I shall be very annoyed if it is not!" the Earl replied.

"Once we are . . . aboard," she said, "we shall . . . be on British . . . soil."

The Earl realised she was working it out for herself and he said:

"That is true, and, as we are no longer at war, we have nothing to fear from other ships in the Channel."

Lynetta gave a deep sigh.

He knew that she was afraid that even at the last moment she might be prevented from leaving France.

Then she slipped her hand into his and, as he took it, bent her head and kissed it.

Her action was so unexpected that it brought the fire into the Earl's eyes.

He put his arms around her and held her against him.

Then he said, "When we reach England, my darling, will you marry me?"

He knew as he spoke that he had made up his mind completely and for all time.

He loved Lynetta; she was everything he wanted in his wife; he could not contemplate life without her.

For a moment she just stared at him.

Then there was a radiance in her face which made her more beautiful than anyone the Earl had ever seen before.

"D-did you . . . ask me to . . . m-marry you?" she whispered.

"I am going to marry you!" the Earl said firmly. "I love you, my precious. Everything about you is perfect, and nothing else in the world is of any consequence."

"That is . . . what I feel about . . . you," Lynetta replied.

He kissed her and it was a reverent kiss, as if he dedicated himself to her for all time.

Then the softness and sweetness of her lips and the way she responded to him made him become more possessive.

He held her closer still and kissed her until they were both breathless.

"I . . . love you . . . I love you!" Lynetta sighed. "I will do . . . everything that I can to make you . . . happy."

"I am blissfully happy now," the Earl said, and it was true.

He knew as they drove through the streets of Calais and down to the Quay that he had made the right decision.

He would do everything necessary to prevent any scandal.

Even though it would mean, he thought, going down on his knees to Elaine to ask her to release him.

He was prepared to give her half his fortune, if necessary.

But whatever the cost, nothing would ever make him give up Lynetta.

If she filled his world, he knew that for her there was nothing else but him.

Because of that, he had to protect her, to look after her and make her happy.

He put his hand under her chin to turn her face up to his.

"I worship you, my darling," he said, "and when we are married I will thank God every day of my life that I found you!"

"As I have thanked ... Him ever ... since you ... saved me."

She put up her hand with its long, slim fingers to touch his cheek.

"I prayed and prayed ... that I would ... escape from ... Ségar," she said, "and ... suddenly in shining armour my Knight was there!"

There was a note of awe in her voice. The Earl knew that for her he was still a Knight with supernatural powers.

It made him feel both humble and proud, and at the same time, vitally aware of his responsibility to her.

Then because there were no words with which to express his feelings, he was kissing her, demandingly, fiercely, and very possessively, as if he was afraid of losing her.

The carriage came to a stop at the Quay, and the Earl looked out for the *Sea Lion*.

She was, he thought, very splendid, her masts silhouetted against the setting sun.

They stepped out, the Earl thanking the coachman and rewarding him handsomely.

He then thanked the Sergeant and then their escort. He shook hands with them.

When Lynetta tried to do the same they took off their helmets and raised her hand to their lips.

The Earl invited them to have a special dinner to celebrate their safe journey and gave them a large sum of money which would more than pay for the meal.

It meant that each soldier would have an extra month's pay in his pocket.

With everybody smiling and bowing, the Earl and Lynetta walked up the gang-plank. The Captain was waiting on deck.

"Welcome back, M'Lord!"

"I am very glad to see you again!" the Earl replied.

Even as he spoke he gave an exclamation. Standing a little behind him was a familiar figure.

"Henry!" the Earl exclaimed.

"Hello, Darrill!" his friend replied. "I hoped you would not keep me waiting too long!"

"What are you doing here?" the Earl questioned.

Then he remembered Lynetta was standing beside him.

"Let me introduce to you my oldest and dearest friend, Henry Lynham," he said. "He has certainly surprised me by being aboard the *Sea Lion!*"

If the Earl was surprised, so was Henry.

He was looking at Lynetta with astonishment.

The Earl knew that he did not miss the beauty of her face or the elegance of her gown and bonnet.

They went into the Saloon, and a steward brought them a bottle of Champagne.

149

"I should like," Lynetta said a little shyly, "to go . . . below and take . . . off my . . . bonnet."

"Yes, of course," the Earl said. "I will show you where you are sleeping."

He took Lynetta down the companionway. He opened the door of a cabin which was next to his own and which was very attractively decorated.

Hunt had already brought down one of Lynetta's trunks and was supervising another which was carried by two seamen.

Lynetta looked at the Earl.

"I think," she said, "if you do not want me for the moment, I would like to lie down for a little while."

"That would be very sensible," the Earl said. "Hunt will unpack for you, and I will tell you if there is any sign of the furniture."

She smiled at him beguilingly.

It was only with difficulty that he was able to leave her and go back to where Henry was already sipping his Champagne.

As he walked into the Saloon and shut the door, Henry said:

"Only you, Darrill, could have found anything so lovely, and so exquisite. Who is she? Is she one of the treasures you are importing to England?"

"She is *the* treasure! The only one that counts!" the Earl said firmly.

He sat down as he spoke.

He drank half the glass of Champagne that was waiting for him and felt he needed it.

Then, as his friend did not speak, he questioned:

"I suppose you have some reason for being here?"

"I came to bring you some bad news," Henry replied, "and I thought you would rather hear it from me than from anybody else."

"What is it?" the Earl asked.

"Elaine is marrying Hampton tomorrow!"

The Earl shut his eyes.

He could hardly believe what he had heard, and yet the Heavens had opened and the angels were singing.

"I was afraid you might be upset," Henry was saying, "but seeing whom you have with you, I am doubtful."

"You have told me what I have been praying for!" the Earl replied.

He spoke so solemnly that his friend stared at him in surprise.

As if he thought he should give his friend time to adjust himself to the news, Henry said:

"As you are not as upset as I thought you might be, I have something to tell you that I think may surprise you."

"What is that?" the Earl asked.

"I discovered when meeting an old friend of the family exactly why Elaine managed to attract you, of all unlikely people, as well as Hampton and a great number of others."

"What are you saying?" the Earl enquired.

"Apparently," Henry went on, "Lady Dale was, when she was a girl in Ireland, an outstanding actress."

He saw the surprise in the Earl's eyes and said quickly: "She was not on the stage, or anything like that, but they used to have Charades in the crumbling Castle which was all her father owned."

"Go on!" the Earl said.

"A member of my family who had seen her perform said she was absolutely outstanding! Far better than Mrs. Siddons or Mrs. Jordan."

The Earl was listening as Henry continued:

"When she married Lord William she was furious to

find that, as a younger son, he had no money, and was determined to see that Elaine did not make the same mistake she had."

"What mistake?" the Earl asked.

"Thinking that a title, even an inferior one, would compensate for being poor!" Henry said bluntly.

The Earl was beginning to see where this story was leading.

"Apparently she taught Elaine almost as soon as she could toddle," Henry went on, "how to get anything she wanted."

He bent forward in his chair as he continued:

"Can you not see, Darrill, how skilfully she instructed and rehearsed Elaine in the devious way by which she managed to intrigue everybody, including you?"

The Earl sat up in his chair.

"Are you telling me the whole thing was an act?"

"Of course it was!" Henry said. "Lady William is very shrewd. She knew that you, for instance, and Hampton have had far too many women falling into your arms like over-ripe peaches to be interested in a young girl!"

The Earl drew in his breath.

"You had to be intrigued and deceived by somebody who appeared indifferent to any advances you might make, and she was clever enough to play two aces off against each other!"

"Dammit! You are making me out a fool!" the Earl exclaimed.

"That is exactly what you were," Henry said. "But you can be excused because Lady William manipulated Elaine like a puppet—very cleverly!"

The Earl did not speak, and Henry finished: "All I

can say is thank God for your sake that she chose Hampton and not you!"

"I am prepared to say 'Amen' to that!" the Earl replied.

He rose to his feet as he spoke and went to the porthole.

Looking up at the sun, crimson and gold against the darkening sky, he thought he was the luckiest man in the world.

Now he had taken his last hurdle and Lynetta could be his wife without any difficulties.

There would be no scandal, no recriminations, no Royal disapproval.

Henry was watching him, a faint smile on his lips.

As he turned round, he asked: "What are you going to do?"

"Get married!" the Earl answered.

Henry stared at him.

"When?"

"Tonight!"

"Tonight?" Henry repeated incredulously.

The Earl returned to his chair.

"I love Lynetta," he said, "and I intended to marry her, whatever the consequences!"

"Elaine might have sued you for Breach of Promise."

"I took that into consideration," the Earl said, "and I also thought I should be exiled from Buckingham Palace and even perhaps have to resign from my Club."

"There is no need for any of that now!" Henry said quickly.

"Yes, I know, but I have no wish to have the members of White's Club think that Hampton has beaten me to the Winning Post. More important, thinking I married Lynetta out of pique."

Henry understood.

"Then what do you intend to do?"

"I intend," the Earl said quietly, "to tell the Captain to take the *Sea Lion* a little way out of the harbour, then Lynetta and I can be married legally—at sea."

Henry's eyes twinkled.

"I understand," he said. "When your marriage is announced it will have taken place the day *before* Elaine marries Hampton!"

"Exactly!" the Earl said. "And actually, whether you believe it or not, I am thinking of Elaine rather than myself."

Henry knew he had been right.

If the Earl married immediately after Elaine, a number of his friends who knew she had sent him to France would be certain he was just trying to hide his chagrin at being thrown over.

"I think it is an excellent idea," he said. "I hope you will permit me to be your Best Man?"

"Who else?" the Earl enquired.

As he spoke, he went from the Saloon to find the Captain.

Three of the seamen were sent into the Town to buy up every flower that was available.

Then he went to his own cabin to enjoy the bath that Hunt had prepared for him.

When he had dried himself he did not at once begin to dress.

Instead he put on the long robe he had worn when he had slept beside Lynetta and went into her cabin.

She was, as he expected, fast asleep.

In the last golden light of the sun before it sank over the horizon, he thought she looked like an angel dropped down from Heaven.

He sat down on the bed, and as he had longed to do before, he kissed her until she woke.

As she did so, instinctively she put her arms around his neck.

His kiss became more possessive and he felt, almost as if it came from the sky outside, a touch of fire in the response of her lips.

He raised his head.

"I . . . I was . . . asleep," she said.

"And looking very lovely, my darling one, but now you have to wake up."

"Is it time for dinner?"

"Yes, and it is early because we have something very important to do afterwards."

"What is that?"

"We are going to be married!"

She stared at him as if she had not heard him aright.

Then she said: "M-married?"

"Yes, my precious, because I love you so over-whelmingly, and because I want to return to England with you as my wife, we are going to be married at sea."

Her eyes seemed to hold a thousand lights in them, but she did not speak, and the Earl said:

"I know, my beloved, you would probably have liked a Church wedding, but, as we have seen on our journey, most of the Churches are in ruins, and I expect those at Calais are the same."

"It . . . it would not matter where I was married," Lynetta whispered, "if it was . . . to you!"

"It will be to me, and you will be my wife legally," the Earl said. "When we reach Charn you can have any Service you like in my own Chapel, which has over the centuries been both Catholic and Protestant."

He looked at her a little anxiously, but she smiled as she said:

"To be married at sea would be . . . very thrilling and . . . unusual."

"Then put on your prettiest gown," the Earl said, "and I will tell Hunt to find you a wedding veil. I am sure it will not be difficult."

Lynetta laughed.

"Everything about you is so exciting," she said. "I never in all my dreams, thought of being . . . married at . . . sea!"

"Well, hurry, and get dressed," the Earl said, "in case the movement of the ship makes you feel seasick."

"That would be very unromantic!" Lynetta said.

He smiled and went to his cabin to dress.

Lynetta found that Hunt had already taken several of her best gowns from her trunk and hung them up to prevent them from becoming creased.

She looked at the gowns she had chosen with Josephine Bonaparte, then took down the one the Earl had liked, which was silver.

It shimmered as she moved.

When she went into the Saloon she knew by the expression in his eyes that the Earl understood why she had chosen it.

He had beside him the box which contained the jewellery he had bought for her in Paris.

When he clasped the necklace round her neck and the bracelets on her wrists she looked, he thought, as if she had come from Olympus.

He kissed the ring, then slipped it on her finger, saying as he did so:

"That is the first chain that binds you to me."

"I do not . . . need a . . . chain," she whispered so that Henry could not hear.

To be tactful, he had walked across to look out of the porthole at the darkening sky.

The stars were coming out in the great arc of the sky.

He thought with delight that he had done the right thing in coming to warn the Earl of what he would hear when he reached England.

He knew better than anyone else that for the Earl to be married before Elaine would enhance his reputation.

He had always been in the lead and it would be unthinkable to let those who were jealous of him think he had taken a fall.

Planning in his mind, Henry knew it would be true to say that the Earl was married at sea because few Churches in France were open and Clergymen were hard to find.

"Darrill has won again!" he told himself triumphantly.

He knew what was more important than anything else was that he had never seen his friend deeply in love.

They knew each other so well that he was aware that the Earl had never really been in love with Elaine.

She had merely constituted a challenge.

That it had all been a contrived plot to ensnare either the Earl or Hampton made it all the better that the Earl should come out on top.

There was still something he had not yet related, because there had not been the opportunity, that the reason why Elaine had sent the Earl to France was to play for time, so as to be sure that the Marquess's father was going to die.

The Duke had been ill for months, but as he was a comparatively young man, there was no reason why he should not recover and live for at least another twenty years.

Lady William had wanted the very best for her

daughter, and what could be better than being a Duchess?

But for the bridegroom to be subsidiary to his father who held the purse-strings was something she had endured for nearly twenty years.

She was determined that Elaine should not experience the same frustration.

"I can tell him all that later," Henry said to himself. "What he wants to think of at the moment is that exquisite creature he has found in France!"

The steward brought in the dinner. It was not a long meal, but a delicious one.

They did not eat in the Saloon, but in another cabin.

The Earl explained he had built it into the yacht as a place for writing and reading.

"It is," he said, "for those who do not want to chatter or be disturbed."

When the last course was finished the Earl looked at Lynetta sitting beside him and she understood what he wanted without putting it into words.

"Shall I go and get . . . ready?" she asked.

She was aware as she spoke that the sails were billowing out and they were catching the very faint breeze which was blowing from the South.

It was a warm night and the sea was calm.

As Lynetta went below to her cabin she knew she need not be afraid of feeling seasick.

What she felt was a wild, irrepressible excitement that she was to marry the Earl and need never be afraid again.

It was hard to believe that she was not dreaming and that she should wake up to find herself in the little cottage terrified to move or speak in case she should be heard or seen.

No, it was true. She was here and very much in love.

"Thank you . . . thank you, God!" she whispered.

Then she saw lying on the bed a lace veil that might have been made by fairy fingers.

She put it over her head, and held it in place by the wreath that lay beside it.

It was made of real flowers: lilies of the valley, syringa, daisies, and others to which she could not put a name.

It was a living copy of her necklace.

She knew that the Earl must have given explicit instructions as to what he required.

She was looking at herself in the mirror, thinking she was now very different from the frightened girl who had hidden in that dark, secret passage at the Château.

There was a knock on the door.

"Come in," she answered.

The door opened and Henry stood there.

"You are ready?" he asked.

He came across the cabin to say: "I am giving you away, and also acting as Darrill's Best man!"

He looked at her for a long moment before he said: "You are very beautiful, and I think you love Darrill."

"I do love him with all my heart," Lynetta said.

"And he loves you," Henry replied, "and because we have always meant so much to each other, I want his happiness more than I want my own."

"I have been praying," Lynetta said, "that I would make him happy, but please . . . will you help me? I am afraid I am very . . . ignorant, having met so few men in my life . . . and none in the . . . last three years."

Henry looked at her in surprise, but he said:

"I hope we will always be friends, and as a friend I will do anything you ask of me."

He took Lynetta's hand and kissed it.

Then he put her arm through his and, without saying

any more, he escorted her up the companionway.

When they reached the top Hunt was there with a bouquet of white flowers which resembled her wreath.

He put it into Lynetta's hand and, when she smiled at him, said:

"Good luck—an' God bless you, M'Lady!"

Henry took her into the Saloon which, since she had last seen it, had been transformed with flowers of every description.

The Earl had, in fact, ordered every blossom that could be found in Calais.

As she came in the Earl thought she did not look like a flower, but rather like the moonlight.

There was something spiritual about her which made her appear to him as if she came from the Heavens rather than from the earth.

He knew, as she stood at his side, that he did indeed worship her.

It was something he would do all his life.

The Captain, looking very smart in his best uniform and medals, read the Marriage Service in a deep voice with an unmistakable sincerity.

Then he finished with the words:

"By the power invested in me by His Majesty King George III, I pronounce you man and wife, and may God bless your union!"

He closed the Prayer Book.

Lynetta looked up at the Earl with an expression of love which transfigured her. Without feeling in the slightest self-conscious he bent his head and kissed her.

"You are now my wife!" he said quietly.

Then, without speaking to either the Captain or to Henry, he put his arm round her.

He drew her across the Saloon and down the companionway.

She thought he was taking her to her cabin, but to her surprise he opened the door of his own, the Master Cabin. It occupied the whole width of the stern.

As she went inside she gave a little gasp.

Two lanterns were lit and they revealed that the whole cabin was decorated with white flowers.

The seamen, on the Earl's instructions, had created a bower.

It was so beautiful and so fragrant that Lynetta gave a cry of delight.

"How could you have done...anything so... lovely?" she asked.

"We have had a rather strange wedding, my darling," the Earl replied, "but I want you to remember it as the most important day of our lives."

She lifted her lips to his, but first he took the wreath from her head, then the veil, and dropped them on a chair.

He undid her necklace and released her hair. It fell over her shoulders, as it had done when she had slept beside him.

He held her close, and as he kissed her, she felt him undoing the back of her gown.

It slithered to the floor and lay there like a pool of moonlight.

Then the Earl lifted her into the bed and she lay among the flowers breathing in the fragrance of them.

The sea was very still with just the lap of the waves against the sides of the yacht.

She thought that everything was enchanted and that she herself was part of a fairy-tale.

The Earl slipped into bed beside her.

As he did so she remembered how she had cried on his shoulder and how afterwards they had lain side by side.

'Why did I not realise . . . then how much I . . . love him?' she asked herself.

Now her heart was beating frantically and she felt sensations, like the moonlight itself, moving through her breasts, up into her throat to quiver on her lips.

"I love you, my beautiful, wonderful little wife!" the Earl said.

"And . . . I love you," Lynetta replied. "How can . . . any man be so . . . magnificent . . . so clever and . . . so kind?"

There was a little break before the last words.

She was thinking how he had not only been kind to her but also to *Mademoiselle* Bernier and the soldiers who had escorted them to Calais.

"We are married!" the Earl exclaimed almost as if he was convincing himself. "Now I know I need no longer have to stop myself from kissing you, because I had no wish to make you more afraid than you were already."

"Did you . . . want to . . . kiss me?"

"It is impossible to tell you how much," he said, "or how agonising it was to lie close to you and not to touch you."

He thought she looked surprised, and knew she did not really understand.

"I adore you, my precious," he said, "but I have no wish to make you afraid of me, or to hurt you in any way."

"How . . . could I be . . . afraid of . . . you?" Lynetta asked.

She looked up at him and added: "When I am . . . close to you like this . . . I know it is the . . . most exciting and . . . wonderful thing that could ever happen to me!"

The way she spoke and her body quivering against

his told the Earl that she was feeling the same rapture and ecstasy as he was.

It was more intense, more wonderful than anything he had ever known.

Because it was impossible to express in words, he kissed Lynetta very gently on her eyes, her lips, then her neck.

She moved beneath him. It intensified what she was feeling already, and it was something she had never known before.

"I love . . . you," she whispered. "Oh, my darling Knight . . . I love you."

"What do you feel?" the Earl asked.

"So wildly excited . . . I cannot . . . breathe . . . and the stars are flickering . . . inside me."

"My precious, my darling, Heart of my Heart, I adore you."

"Teach me . . . about love . . . I was so afraid . . . I would never . . . find love."

"I will teach you to love me."

"I love you . . . already with . . . all of me . . . my heart and my soul . . . are yours."

"And your beautiful body?"

"That is . . . yours . . . if you . . . want it."

"Want it?" The Earl's voice was very deep. "My precious wife, I want it—unbearably . . ."

"Then show me . . . tell me . . . teach me what . . . to do."

"I worship you!"

As the scent of flowers enveloped them and the stars came out overhead, the Earl knew they were flying into the sky. They were no longer human, but Divine.

He had found the treasure which all men seek and so

few find. It was when two people who were brought together by God became one.

He had blessed them in this life and in the life that would come after it. They were with Him in the splendour, the wonder, and Glory of Love.

Barbara Cartland, the world's most famous romantic novelist, who is also an historian, playwright, lecturer, political speaker and television personality, has now written over 460 books and sold nearly 500 million copies all over the world.

She has also had many historical works published and has written four autobiographies as well as the biographies of her mother and that of her brother, Ronald Cartland, who was the first Member of Parliament to be killed in the last war. This book has a preface by Sir Winston Churchill and has just been republished with an introduction by Sir Arthur Bryant.

Love at the Helm, a novel written with the help and inspiration of the late Earl Mountbatten of Burma, Great Uncle of His Royal Highness The Prince of Wales, is being sold for the Mountbatten Memorial Trust.

She has broken the world record for the last

twelve years by writing an average of twenty-three books a year. In the Guinness Book of Records she is listed as the world's top-selling author.

Miss Cartland in 1978 sang an Album of Love Songs with the Royal Philharmonic Orchestra.

In 1964 Barbara Cartland founded the National Association for Health of which she is the President, as a front for all the Health Stores and for any product made as alternative medicine.

This is now a £300,000 turnover a year, with one third going in export.

In January 1988 she received "La Médaille de Vermeil de la Ville de Paris." This is the highest award to be given in France by the City of Paris.

BARBARA CARTLAND

Called after her own
beloved Camfield Place,
each Camfield Novel of Love
by Barbara Cartland
is a thrilling, never-before published
love story by the greatest romance
writer of all time.

May '89...REVENGE IS SWEET
June '89...THE PASSIONATE PRINCESS
July '89...SOLITA AND THE SPIES

79